Ski Lovers

James DuBern

Huspel

Chapter One

♥

As the lift door pinged, a small cheer erupted from a group of party-goers. Against a hum of chatter and mellow house music, Emma swirled into the penthouse in a dress that shimmered blue-green like a peacock. Wavy cocoa hair hovered weightlessly on her shoulders, framing a pretty face with sharp cheekbones and cute dimples around her smile.

"Wow," Kendal said, looking his girlfriend up and down. "You look stunning."

Emma batted her eyelashes playfully, lifting her skirt as she stepped out of the lift. The spotlights flashed a reflection on the toe of her polished black boots.

"Why thank you, sir. You scrub up pretty well yourself," she said.

The party's host carried himself with regal confidence. He had modelled, briefly, in his university days. Emma kept copies of clothing catalogues in which he was joyfully rowing a boat or brooding with a polo club on his shoulder. For Kendal, it was barely work. Tonight, he wore a black tux, and his blond hair was swept back as if he had sky-dived onto the terrace. Emma touched it affectionately and found it oddly firm. "Like a Lego Minifigure," she joked.

"Did you bring heels?" he asked, nosing in her tote bag and motioning to a waiter to take it from her hands.

Emma gently bit her upper lip.

"Long day at the office. I couldn't face heels. Anyway, I thought these were cute."

She lifted her leg, revealing a lace up boot with a chunky sole and eyelets up to just above the ankle. Kendall managed a smile.

"Didn't you tell them you had a party to get to?" he frowned. They paused beneath a chandelier that splashed diamond-shaped sparkles onto the walnut flooring. A party-goer floated by, head weaving this way and that. Kendal pointed in the direction of a bathroom and they scurried off with a look of relief.

"As you know, my social life isn't Nigel's biggest concern. Kendal, you know I'm just starting out. It won't be forever," Emma continued, with a neutral smile.

"She says, *forever*. I just think, why bother? Do you need the stress of a job?" Kendal argued.

"Not tonight," Emma said, touching his cheek with the side of her index finger.

He sighed and changed the subject. "You're right. We should enjoy the housewarming."

Kendal surveyed his expansive penthouse, the grin returning to his jawline, head nodding to the beat. "And your birthday," he added.

Emma laughed at his late correction.

"Kendal, I could have shown up naked and nobody would notice me tonight. Your new pad is tonight's headliner, and rightly so," she said, her eyes drinking in the opulent decor. "I want a tour! The spotlights were hanging from the ceiling when I last saw it. There were cables everywhere."

"Ah yes. You'll be pleased to know that I took your advice and insisted they put a plug socket in the middle of the floor."

"You'll thank me when you try to hoover this vast place."

Kendal snorted.

"Okay okay," she corrected herself "Your mum will thank me."

He was about to lead her into the thicket of guests when the lift doors opened once again, revealing another couple. He, a beaming smile in a sharp black suit and her, shiny hair and skyscraper heels, bursting out of a black cocktail dress with glittering diamonds around her neck. Emma noted Kendal's eye-bulging glee but ignored the discomfort growing in her stomach. Bella looked spectacular - who wouldn't stare?

"Charlie, Bella!" the host said, detaching himself from Emma to greet his guests.

Kendal gently tugged the tail of a burgundy scarf and Charlie rotated, arms out like a scarecrow, to allow it to uncoil. Kendal set about locating drinks, as if his guests had staggered in from a desert marathon and needed urgent rehydration. Emma returned Bella's cheek kiss and compliments, grateful to see some familiar faces.

Kendal folded the scarf over the arm of a server and took three glasses of champagne for his guests of honour.

"To eight months of decorators, architects, and signing cheques until my wrist hurt," he said. Emma raised her glass and repeated the toast.

"And of course, to the birthday girl," Charlie added, with a nod to Emma, who smiled in response.

The foursome finally set off through Kendal's newly acquired penthouse, hands linked, sewing their way through a crowd of slick city types. The bedrooms looked copy-pasted from a high-end hotel, down to the built-in bedside tables and softly lit wooden slats that lined the wall. *Dust traps*, Emma thought, immediately disappointing herself for being so boringly practical. This was, in any case, not a man who dusts. Kendal's office was dark and moody, with a chair so central it looked like a throne. Emma sat on it, swinging this way and that, and running her hands across the burgundy leather that topped the desk.

"This is strong, Kendal," she said. "But to complete the Bond villain look, you need a cat. And one of those globes that opens up to reveal a decanter of brandy. Perhaps a gun. Or a nuclear button."

"Never getting a cat," he said. "But the nuke thing, I like that."

"You seem so well read, Kendal," teased Charlie, motioning to the floor to ceiling bookcases that remained starkly empty.

"Yes, I know, I know," he said, holding the door open to usher the tour back into the main room. "I just don't read books anymore. I use an e-reader. Come and see the kitchen!"

Emma looked at Bella and suppressed a smile.

"E-reader," Emma mouthed. "He has Kendal Unlimited."

Bella slapped her hand.

The kitchen was all sleek black cabinetry behind a curved marble island. A guest stood quickly from a barstool to greet the host, who smiled graciously and said he would return shortly.

"Italian marble, no doubt?" Emma said, running her fingertips on the bevelled edge. "You have to be careful with wine, I think."

Kendal shrugged.

"If anyone is careful with wine, I will have them ejected. Honestly, I don't know where it's from; I didn't choose any of it. The designer kept emailing me options and I just told her to make it look like a magazine. She said, 'what magazine?'"

He laughed.

"To be fair, Kendal, that is a fairly vague design brief. There are lots of magazines," Emma said.

Kendal stopped at the fridge, and a couple of people moved out of the way so he could open its barn-sized door.

"Really, though? I'm not going to want it looking like *Farmer's Weekly*, am I?"

"Oy!" she said. "Nothing wrong with a good farmhouse."

Charlie crouched by the fridge, eyeing its contents with admiration. Bottles stacked until the shelves bowed. Platters of sushi under cling film blankets.

"Where are the leftover takeaways and mouldy condiments?" he asked, with a tut and shake of the head. "You've changed, Kendal."

"I haven't changed one jot, Charlie boy. I just finish my takeaways like a real man."

The tour continued into a sunken nook lined with sofas. Bolted to the wall that separated the lounge and kitchen was a graffiti mural of a rat holding a roadworks sign.

"Is that a real Banksy?" Charlie asked, feeling the rough edges of the thick concrete slab.

Kendal looked at his old friend and followed his eyes to the wall, as if he'd forgotten the artwork was there. He nodded, then reached out a hand and set off once again. Charlie followed obediently, half-looking back.

"I didn't know you could buy them. Isn't he all anti-capitalist?" Charlie asked.

"Everyone has a price," Kendal called back. "Even Banksy."

The group breezed past an ornamental grand piano with not a fingerprint on its glossy black surface.

"Can you play?" Bella asked.

"Of course not," Kendal said. "But nothing says success like wasting space in central London. That's what my designer said."

Finally, they had reached the main selling point of the property, the floor to ceiling glass that overlooked the Thames. Kendal slid a door open and guests diffused onto the terrace. Emma felt a shiver of adrenaline as she soaked up the incredible view. Tower Bridge was spectacularly lit, like a pair of fairytale castles ready to soar into the sky. She leaned over the railing and swallowed her nerves to look at the riverside promenade below. Couples wrapped up in fur-hooded parkas drank hot chocolate as they ambled along the Thames Path. To the left, she could make out the Millennium Bridge, lit baby blue against the black water.

The four of them lined up, elbows on the thick glass wall that secured them in their palatial crow's nest.

"I'll never get bored of that view," Kendal said, wistfully.

"Kendal, you really are the luckiest man alive," Charlie said.

Emma pulled her boyfriend toward her and lowered her head into his shoulder.

"I'm the lucky one," she said with a sigh. "Two years ago we were in a bed in a hostel in Vietnam. Cockroaches on the pillow. Now this."

Kendal gave her a gentle squeeze and then broke away from the embrace.

"Okay, I'm bored," he said. "I've got something I need to take care of. Emma, do you have a drink?"

She held up her champagne glass and smiled. He nodded eagerly, and she realised he was actually waiting for her to take a sip, which she did.

Emma watched him buzz into the thicket of friends and hangers-on he had accumulated in his two years of post-university life. She watched him slap backs and chink glasses with a group of guys from his investment bank, unsure if she knew them or not. She subtly tipped her drink into a plant pot.

"I bet he's humblebragging about having to buy two car spaces to fit his Porsche," Charlie said.

"You know him too well," Emma replied, turning back to the river view. Below them sat the HMS Belfast, a hulking metal warship that looked like a toy from this height.

"Oh, you see that magnolia tree?" Emma said excitedly, setting down her empty flute.

"What's a magnolia?" Bella said. "It sounds very eighties."

Emma pointed at a tree growing out of a wide pavement on the opposite side of the river. Its leaves had long since dropped for winter and its naked branches were silhouetted against a passing double-decker bus.

"There, the one with a spiked fence around the base, like a crown for a king. It's gorgeous. It was in bloom in spring when we first looked at this place. There's another really beautiful plane tree just up the river. Oldest one in the city. I dragged Kendal to it the other day."

"I bet he was fascinated," said Charlie.

Emma elbowed him.

"Do you know a lot about the city?" asked Bella.

"No; I still get lost on the underground," Emma said. "I just like trees. There are eight million of them in London. One for each of us residents."

"Is that one yours?" said Bella.

Emma nodded proudly.

"So, are you two living together, finally?" Bella asked as they turned away from the window.

"No. Maybe soon."

"You can't do much better than this place," Charlie said.

"I know. It's gorgeous, and Kendal was very sweet about allotting me wardrobe space. I'm still happy with my own place, you know?"

Bella shrugged.

"You'll be like us soon enough, feet up on the coffee table, arguing about what to watch on Netflix," she said, looking to her boyfriend for a laugh.

Charlie was too busy eyeing up the lounge area with its sumptuous, colourful sofas. "Seriously though, don't tell me Kendal doesn't have a TV?" he said.

Emma pointed at the floor, where a slim rectangle marked a subtle outline in the iroko flooring.

"Of course," he said.

The music stopped, exposing a buzz of chatter. At the ting of a fork against a thin glass flute, Emma, Charlie, and Bella returned to the warmth of the apartment. The crowd parted, leaving a valley between the kitchen and the windows where Emma was framed dramatically by the open door. Kendal pushed a trolley toward her, upon which was an enormous cake in the shape of a mountain.

"Happy birthday to you," he sang. The rest of the guests joined in, staring excitedly at a reddening Emma. She bit her lip nervously, hoping the song wouldn't make way for rounds of hip hip hoorays. Dozens of phones were raised, and Emma kept a smile fixed on her face for the appropriate length of time.She dutifully blew out the candles, the crowd cheered, and she resumed her breathing when the music picked up.

"Thank you, Kendal," she said, pulling back her hair as she leaned over the cake to give him a kiss.

"Where's your drink?" Kendal asked.

"Why are you trying to get me drunk, I wonder?" She asked with a laugh. "I finished it." Again, her boyfriend's eyes darted around for assistance, and Emma's hand restocked with an impossibly delicate glass. She crouched to examine the conical mound of chocolate sponge with rivers of white icing snaking from peak to base. On closer inspection she saw tiny skiers dotted over the pistes, and a ski lift made of plastic and string.

"It works, too!" Kendal said with boyish excitement. The red, matchbox-sized gondola whirred into life, climbing slowly up the wire parallel to the slope.

She looked at her boyfriend quizzically.

"Kendal, it's beautiful," she said. "And practical, of course. The little skiers have to be able to reach the top. But ...was there a mix up at the bakery or something?"

Kendal coughed loudly, drawing the attention of those in earshot. He pulled a fan of cardboard slips from his back pocket.

"Pack your skis. We're going to Switzerland!" he announced. A cheer went up around him.

"Wow! Really?" she replied. "When?"

"Monday."

Charlie and Bella laughed.

"This Monday? Like, the day after tomorrow?" Emma said, looking at the tickets and double-checking the date on her watch. "Oh, yes. Monday. But what about my job? I've got mountains of work. No pun intended."

Kendal swept away her concerns with a wave of his hand.

"Don't worry. You can do it when you're back. I messaged Anthony; he cleared your diary."

"Really? I don't know how you managed to convince them to let me leave. And my dad! I'm meant to see him next weekend. And the outfit. Those trousers with the braces. Goggles!?"

Emma sat on the arm of a sofa, taking it all in. Bella chuckled, placing a reassuring hand on her wrist.

"Salopettes. Don't worry Emma, it's going to be so much fun!"

"Were you in on it?" Emma asked.

"Well, we're coming, so..."

"Yay!" Emma squeaked. "Okay, I need you to hold my hand the entire time while I'm learning. Like, the whole week. I am a klutz."

"Learning what?" Bella asked with a laugh.

"How to ski. I've never been before."

"Oh - I didn't realise. Kendal didn't mention that." Bella glanced over to where their host was entertaining a group of guests. "I'm sure he has lessons planned. You're going to love it. It'll be fun!"

"It'll be fun," Emma repeated quietly, looking down at the toes of her boots.

Bella stroked her arm reassuringly and then joined in the group hovering around Kendal, chiming in with the part she played in planning the surprise. Emma stood for a moment, drink in hand, smiling politely as a guest bumped into her on their way to snap the cake.

A notification pinged on Emma's phone, which she hurriedly silenced. A meeting had appeared on her calendar at one-o-clock in the morning. With her screen discreetly at hip height, she did a double-take at the uninvited lozenge of pixels that had burst into existence like a volcanic island in a calm sea. It was followed up by a text message from her boss, Nigel, unapologetically requiring her attendance. Emma glanced over at Kendal, making sure he was occupied before slipping away to the main bedroom.

Head spinning, she shut the door behind her and tipped her drink into the ensuite sink. She sat on the bed and gathered her thoughts, looking at her reflection in the floor to ceiling mirror. Not wanting to invite existential introspection which would inevitably ruin her make-up, she slid the doors open and took a quiet moment to unpack her belongings.

Kendal's tailored suits filled a wardrobe, a great expanse of thundercloud grey for a world where it rained money. At the foot were his trademark tan leather brogues, pair after indistinguishable pair. A single drawer was left conspicuously empty, and she set about unpacking the few items she had brought. She flattened out the bra and socks, spacing them out to make it look properly occupied.

With the buzz of the party outside the bedroom door, she fired up her laptop. Despite Kendal's assurance, her calendar remained packed like a Mondrian painting, with meetings from 7am and ending as late as midnight. She hammered out an email to her assistant, Anthony, but looked at her watch and decided to leave it unsent until the morning. Kendal entered the bedroom, and she partially closed the lid.

"Ah, there you are," he said, noticing the glow from her screen. She shut it the rest of the way. "We're having cake. Are you okay?"

She flopped back on the bed.

"Yes. I am. And I really don't want to seem ungrateful. It's just a lot to take in. I like being organised, you know. I'm not very good with surprises. If I'd have known we were going skiing, I would have done some lessons, and bought the gear."

He sat next to her, stroking her hair gently.

"Don't worry about a thing. Skiing is like riding a bike."

She rolled over and propped herself up with an elbow.

"Kendal, you know that phrase is about how easy it is to recall something you've learned before, even if it was a long time ago?"

He narrowed his eyes for a moment, then laughed.

"You've *never* been skiing?" he exclaimed.

"No. Is that so weird?"

"What holidays did your family do in winter, then, Mauritius? Dubai?"

She shook her head.

"Winter's busy on a farm. We brought the sheep in. Cut firewood."

"Eww," he said, rubbing the back of his neck, his face a look of pained shock. "Let's go and eat that cake. You had cake, right?"

"Smashing party, eh?" Kendal said. He interlocked his fingers behind his head and propped his tired feet on a pouffe that looked like a giant ball of wool. Emma nuzzled in beside him, her boots sat neatly at the side of the couch.

"It was brilliant, thank you," she said. "You really do spoil me."

Emma checked her phone. Ten minutes until her meeting began.

"Did you post the cake on Instagram?" Kendal asked excitedly, launching the app and searching for mentions of himself.

Emma shook her head. "I didn't use my phone all evening."

"I'll ping some to you," he said. "Guess you were busy with work, anyway."

She looked at her watch and sat up, ignoring the petulant tone in his voice. "It's almost one o'clock. I must turn in."

"Are you going to bring your laptop on holiday?" he asked.

"I have to," she said. "There's a big new client, I've told you this. All hands on deck."

"Surely they can live without you for a week," he said.

"Business never sleeps," she said, tapping his leg playfully. She looked at her watch again and yawned.

"Well, I do sleep, and on that note..." he said.

Kendal stood, finally, proudly surveying the glasses and beer bottles that lined every surface of his apartment. Emma remained on the sofa.

"I'm just going to take one last look at the view. I'll join you in a minute," she called after him as he headed for his bedroom.

Emma listened for the sound of an electric toothbrush, then pulled her laptop from beneath the couch. She darted into Kendal's office and kicked the door shut, pulling her hair back into a ponytail. She sat in Kendal's chair and angled her laptop screen, checking that no glasses or party detritus was in shot. The browser seemed to take forever to refresh, despite her thunderous tapping of the 'Join Meeting' button.

A grid of faces burst onto the screen, and the word 'hello' rang five times at once from the laptop's tinny speakers. She could just make out some Germanic accents.

"This is Emma from Dallier and Grayson," she said.

"You also work late over in London," said a greying man in a salmon pink shirt. "Let's begin."

Emma smiled. A private message popped up from her boss.

'*4 mins late.*'

She wanted to type '*It's 1 am on Saturday night. It's my birthday. My boyfriend threw me a party which I didn't even drink at.*' But she wrote just five letters. *Sorry.*

The smiles and nods dragged on for twenty minutes, during which various parties agreed to send follow-up materials, to be treated with the strictest confidence. Why it required a dramatic mid-weekend call was beyond Emma, but clearly her boss was eager to demonstrate that his staff - like him - were sleepless robots. The client, a pharmaceutical giant with operations in fifty countries, was under fire and needed some legal cover.

After some awkward waving, Emma pressed the call end button and closed her laptop.

Emma thumbed through photos of the party, picking out a shot of her and Kendal on the terrace. She tapped a message to her mum.

'*Kendal threw me a party. Great night. Late meeting with work. Just ended! Hopefully in line for promotion, so will be worth it. xx*'

She hit send and crept into the bedroom, where Kendal was fast asleep.

Chapter Two

♥

E mma straddled Kendal's hips, her hands gripping the lapels of the shirt he had failed to remove before bed. He prised open his eyes and grimaced at the clock on his nightstand. Not even seven. Kendal opened and closed his mouth, making a grim sticky noise that sounded like a cat lapping up a puddle.

"You're keen," he croaked, fumbling around for a glass of water.

"Finally. I was starting to think you were dead," Emma said, swinging her leg off him. "We've got a problem."

He hauled himself up against the headboard.

"My passport. It's at my dad's," she said.

His head lolled forward with a groan, his neck muscles declining to participate before the task was even set out.

"It's only two and a half hours each way. We can do this," she said. "We have to do this."

Emma hopped down from the bed. She was already dressed and ready to go, in a pair of jeans and cardigan she had stuffed in her overnight bag.

Kendal slithered back onto the mattress and pulled the duvet over his head. A caterpillar into its chrysalis.

"I can't do it," he said, voice muffled by the covers. "Absolutely not. I'm a hundred times over the limit."

Emma uncovered his face and leaned in to softly kiss his stubble.

"You can, Kendal. I'll make you some nice coffee. We can stop at the services and get a bacon sandwich. It'll be a nice day out in the countryside."

He visibly shuddered.

"You go, Emma. *You* can do this. I'll make *you* some nice coffee, and so on. I'll even make you a little packed lunch of leftover sushi. But I'm not leaving this bed."

"Then I can't go to Switzerland," she said, folding her arms. "You know I don't have a car."

Kendal reached a hand out of his cave and foraged around until it met the metallic clatter of keys. He swung them toward Emma, but she wasn't in the right place and they were sent to the floor.

"Take it," he said. "You're on my insurance.."

"Are you going to show me how to do the gears?" she said.

"It's automatic."

There was a long pause as Emma thought through the prospect of driving Kendal's car up to the farm. *Why not?* She thought.

"Alright, I'm off," she said. "Keep your phone on in case I need a driving lesson. That car is a little much compared to the Mini that I learned in."

"Don't floor it," he said.

"Ya think?" she replied.

Emma repacked her tote bag, double-checking to make sure she had included her laptop and charger, and set it by door to the lift. She turned to say goodbye to Kendal, but he remained motionless, so she closed the bedroom door gently behind her.

Emma took the lift down to the basement, where Kendal's car was parked obnoxiously across his two spaces. She looked at the vehicle and swallowed.

"It's okay," she muttered to herself. "It's just a car. A funny shaped car."

The black Porsche lay low in the dark concrete parking garage, a dragon asleep in its lair. She turned the key fob over in her hands, looking for a button, but then found that merely approaching it awakened the beast. Lights on, eyes open. Emma climbed into the black leather seat, her bum sinking so low that it felt like sitting in a bath. Nervously, she pressed a button on the dash and the vehicle rumbled into life.

She clunked the seatbelt into place and yanked on it to check it would hold her, in the not unimaginable scenario of her spinning out of control down the M11. With great trepidation, she held down the brake, put it into auto and pulled out of the parking space.

Central London was no place for a vehicle that seemed desperate to launch into the horizon. But with a steady foot and determined grip on the wheel, she made her way over Tower Bridge and toward the North Circular. It being the weekend, the financial district was quiet, and by the time she reached the busier intersections where London mellowed into Essex, she found herself singing along to the radio.

At a motorway services, she extracted herself from the beast and relearned to walk. Her awkward gait only added to the unwanted attention she got from a passer by, who looked her up and down and propped his sunglasses on his head.

"Nice car," he said. "Is it yours?"

"Yes," Emma replied, unwilling to let down all of womankind by admitting it was her boyfriend's. Anyway, it was hers today. As the man entered the shop to pay, Emma snuck a little selfie with the car and pinged it to her mum. "New wheels," she said.

On the motorway, she couldn't help but become attached to the vehicle, as it growled past anyone and everyone who dared get in its path. She set a record time as she pulled into the farm track before 10am.

· ♥ · ♥ · ♥ · ♥ · ♥ ·

"Would have been even earlier if I hadn't got stuck behind a tractor," Emma said.

"Good! Someone needs to slow you down in that thing," her father joked, stepping down from the cab of a grain mover. She lowered a paper shopping bag onto the ground and stepped toward her father, hesitating for a moment before throwing her arms around him. She rested her cheek on his shoulder, and then withdrew it when a length of straw stuck to her lips.

"You smell like a farmyard," she said.

"Well, who'd have thought? You smell like..." Michael lowered his large, red nose toward her blond hair and inhaled. "No, I don't know. I can only smell the farm. London hasn't got you yet."

A border collie weaved around Emma's legs in a dizzying figure of eight. She crouched to ruffle his muzzle.

"He's grown," she said.

"That's what they do. Let's put the kettle on," he beamed. "Are you staying for lunch? Marley and the girls are coming."

"No, I must get back," she said.

He smiled, sadly, as he kicked the wellingtons from his feet.

"Work tomorrow?" he asked.

"Actually, Switzerland. I came to pick up my passport. And I can't see you next weekend as planned."

Michael said "Oooh la la," as he dipped his head to avoid the oak beam that separated the lounge and kitchen. The cupboards were a pastel blue, which had come in and out of fashion several times since it was painted when Emma was tiny. On the worktop sat a plate of scones under a glass bell dome.

"Would you like one?" Michael asked as he filled the kettle.

"No, thanks. I'm all caked out. Last night we had a party at Kendal's apartment. We ate a mountain of cake. Literally."

She leaned against the kitchen counter and thumbed through her phone for a photograph, but her father was distracted.

"You reminded me," he said. "Wait there!"

Emma noticed a text message from her boss had come in during her drive, asking curtly if she had seen the emails. She replied, '*Looking now*,' and discovered a stomach-dropping stack of unread messages. The subject lines were mundane *'Private and Confidential'*, and the little paperclip indicated they each had attachments. So much weight carried by that tiny graphic. She set it face down on the wooden worktop as her dad returned with a package wrapped in brown paper. She squeezed it gently.

"Is it a cat?"

She shook it violently, excited as a kid at Christmas.

"I've told you; until you learn not to shake them, you're not getting a kitten," he joked. "But seriously though, take one of ours. They'd have a field day looking for rats in London. Speaking of which, how's Kendal?"

She glared at her father with raised eyebrows, and he chuckled so hard he wheezed.

"Speaking of *London*," he reiterated. "Not speaking of *rats*."

Emma touched the back of a wooden chair, but then remembered her childhood seat on the upholstered bench that hugged the window. The floral fabric had faded but remained one of the many reminders of her mother's touch in the old farmhouse. Emma shimmied in and unwrapped the parcel. Michael poured out the tea, slopping boiling water onto the worktop because he didn't want to miss a second of her reaction.

As the paper opened, she saw thick strands of wool, pale grey and so soft it barely registered against her touch. She lifted it up and a pale jumper unfurled from its shoulders. Emma extracted herself from the bench seat and held it up to her neck, drawing the sleeves out to her wrists. She looked inside the neck and found no label.

"It's gorgeous. Where did you get it?" she asked.

"I made it," he said with pride that burst from him like sunshine.

She narrowed her eyes.

"You made a jumper. You can knit?" she asked, ever the lawyer seeking to confirm the facts.

"I can indeed. You know the fabric shop in Westingbury? I've been selling wool to them for twenty years. Well, the lady there - Natasha - we got chatting, and she gave me some lessons. I must confess, she did the yoke."

Emma hurriedly removed the fleece she was wearing and pulled the sweater over her head.

"The yoke?" she asked, as her head popped through.

"That's what us professionals call the neck," he said.

Emma examined the jumper with wonder, stroking it like a long-lost pet, trying to marry the thought of her father's rough hands with the delicate manipulation of knitting needles.

"You made it?" she asked again, turning this way and that to admire herself in the hallway mirror.

He laughed and nodded.

"I love it. Thank you so much. It must have taken hours and hours."

"Got me out of the house," he said.

Emma was distracted by a ping from her phone. Her boss was again asking if she had seen the emails. She squeezed back into the bench seat, protecting the wool from catching on the underside of the pine dining table, then slid the sleeves up her forearms before lifting her mug of tea. Her father chuckled.

"So, you made it at the wool shop? Was it a course?" she dug.

"Actually, Natasha and I, we..."

His voice tailed off and his cheeks went red. It was Emma's turn to chuckle.

"Made sweet jumpers together?" she teased.

"Something like that," he said, turning his back to her. "Anyway, want a scone?"

"Stop trying to feed me!" she said. Then, "Yes, actually."

He brought the platter to the table and lifted the glass lid. She took a scone and bit into it. He motioned towards the fridge and muttered something about cream, to which Emma politely declined.

"Don't tell me you've started baking too? Or is this Natasha's handiwork?" she asked between bites.

"Marley's kids made these," he said. "You should stay, you haven't seen them since Christmas."

"I can't, Dad. I have to pack for Switzerland. We're going skiing. Kendal bought it for my birthday."

"How is he?"

"The rat?" she joked.

Michael smiled politely and sipped his tea. Emma felt a chill in the air.

"Dad, you don't have to worry about me," she said.

"It's not you I worry about."

"Okay, you know what I mean. You don't have to worry about us. We're good. I want you to come and see Kendal's new flat. You can literally look down on HMS Belfast."

He looked out of the window, past his daughter's head.

"Yes, you said. It sounds lovely. I must come to the city one day."

"You won't, though," she said, putting the remains of her scone on the plate and nudging it forward. He shrugged, apologetically, then gobbled up the leftovers.

"Cities, love. They're just not me. They leave me cold. But I'm happy for you and Kendal. Tell him I said hello. Remind him I've got a shotgun."

She practically spat out her mouthful of tea.

"Did I say that out loud?" he joked. "Oooh, come with me! I've got an idea."

He bounced out of his seat and sped out of the house. Such was his urgency that he wore slippers out in the rain, dodging puddles on the way to a barn.

"Wait!" she said, pausing at the front door. "I need to change my jumper. I don't want to get it wet."

"Don't be daft," he called back. "It's wool. Do you see my sheep worrying about getting wet?"

"That's what we call a non-sequitur," she said, jogging to catch up with her hands shielding her eyes from the rain.

Inside a tumbledown outbuilding, Michael led the way through a workshop that smelled of oil and faintly, mould. Thick wooden workbenches bearing decades of nicks and cuts were piled with pistons and secateurs and spanners and springs.

"Uh oh. Is this the part where you try to teach me how engines work?" she said.

Michael was already halfway up a ladder with his head through a loft hatch. He disappeared up there completely and the ceiling creaked, worryingly. He gave a yelp of excitement and moments later Emma watched some wood emerge through the hatch. She stood at the foot of the ladder to take it from him.

"Ta da!" he said, returning to ground level.

"The sledge!" Emma replied. She brushed a cobweb that bridged the wooden slats of its seat, and untied the long leather strap that linked the front runners.

"Remember when me and Mum did the jump out on Barrow's Hill?" she said.

"Remember?" he said. "I still have nightmares about it. You two bombing down that hill at a hundred miles an hour, and I'm thinking 'for the love of god, roll off before you hit that jump'. Did you roll off? Did you heck!"

They roared with laughter and ran back to the house. Emma used several sheets of kitchen roll to get the dust from the toboggan, each one colouring red with rust.

"Do you think I should take it to Switzerland?" she asked. "Is that what people do on ski holidays?"

"Of course!" he said. "What else are you going to do on a ski holiday?"

"Ski?" she suggested.

"And after skiing?"

"Apres ski?" she said.

"Sledging!"

"Okay, okay, I'll take the sledge. It'll be like old times. Except no you, or Marley. And…"

Her sentence tailed off. Michael put a huge paw onto his daughter's shoulder, his rough skin barbing on the soft wool of her jumper. She squeezed it closer.

With considerable difficulty, they squeezed the toboggan into the boot of Kendal's Porsche. Emma was fumbling through her bag in search of the keys when a battered family estate rumbled down the driveway toward them. A door swung open so hard it bounced against the hinge stop. "Mind the puddle!", came a voice from the driver's seat. Too late. A pair of tiny pink wellies swung out and immediately submerged up to the ankle.

"Auntie Emma!" cried Marley's eldest daughter. "Are you staying for tea? I made scones."

Emma crouched down, glancing briefly at her father.

"Of course. And I must confess, I have already had one," she said.

Several hours later, Emma's phone had collected one missed call from Kendal and two from work. The log fire crackled while her delighted family played a game where they marked their foreheads with a charred wine cork. Emma looked at her watch and pulled back the curtains to peak outside. It was pitch black and the wind howled. She snapped the curtain shut.

"Dad, I'm going to stay, after all, if that's okay. I've got my jacket and overnight bag, and I'll ask Kendal to bring my laptop to the airport."

The family clapped with excitement and the game continued. Emma's father reached an arm around his daughter's shoulder and pulled her in, but she noticed his hands were filthy with charcoal dust.

"Not the jumper!" she shrieked, unfurling his fingers.

Emma held the bannister carefully as she made her way up the creaky stairs to the loft room. The single bed had been lovingly made up by her dad, curtains closed, and radiator cranked up to five. It smelled slightly of burning dust, as rooms do when they haven't been heated for months, and Emma opened the window to the first notch.

With each trip back to the farm, her childhood room felt more alien. During breaks from university, it had been a sanctuary of homeliness which she had rushed to like a child into her father's arms. As the years passed, the narrow bed seemed more fit for the girl she had been than the woman she had become. And now, having lived on her own for two years, the room felt like a museum of her geeky teenage life.

She wiped the dust from the top of her iPod dock, which had seemed so impossibly futuristic when she was twelve but already would be a collector's piece. A pinboard excitedly tracked her progress to becoming a lawyer. A literal rocket cut from Christmas cards sat in its centre, its giveaway crease across the middle.

EM01 written on the side and flaps of red and orange tissue paper gave it an explosive tail. GCSEs, A-levels, and degree had all been ticked off, the tiny dashes of ink doing no justice to the thousands of hours of work involved.

Emma got herself ready for bed, set her alarm for a time so early it made her wince, and put her passport, boarding pass, and car key together for a quick getaway. Her boss sent a text, which he had a habit of doing when she didn't pounce on his emails. She made sure to reply quickly to the texts, in case the next step was him showing up at her bedroom door.

'*Meet first thing,*' it said.

She inhaled deeply to calm herself. There was no easy way of wording this.

'*I'm on holiday this week. Switzerland. Kendal booked it with Anthony. Surprise. Sorry,*' she replied.

'*???*'

'*I'll have my laptop, will review the documents ASAP*', she said.

She stared for several minutes at the blank space where a normal human being might have replied to wish her a safe flight, or a ski emoji. Nothing. She muted her phone and tossed it onto the carpet so she would not be tempted to keep checking it.

The pitch black made her feel anxious, and she opened the door a crack. Hopefully a cat would slink in during the night and keep her company. She used to love waking up to find a feline friend nesting in the crook of her legs. Emma could just about make out her career rocket, its foil fins glinting in the low light. Such determined planning from a teenager, despite her grieving for her mother. With the benefit of age, she could see now that it wasn't despite, but because. Only a rigid plan, a razor-straight launch procedure could have kept her focus on the sky above and not the darkness behind her.

But even the most resolute teenager could only plan so far. Beyond the words 'Emma is Qualified Lawyer!', which of course had the biggest, proudest tick of all, was empty space. An unpinned expanse of cork which had once seemed full of possibility but now felt bewildering and other-worldly. Become a grown up. Task failed successfully. She retrieved her phone from the floor and tapped out a message to her mum.

'Home ain't the same without you, but it's still home. Love you to the moon and back.'

Chapter Three

♥

If you weren't a banker or a skier, you were on the wrong plane. The Swiss Air flight from Heathrow to Zurich was so laden with money that it was a miracle it could get airborne. Millionaires nervously watched their skis being slung into the hold as it sat on the tarmac. As a banker *and* a skier, Kendal was right at home, in business class. He leafed through the glossy seat back magazine and paused on an advert for a silver watch, holding it up against his wrist.

"You do love a Rolex," said Charlie, leaning over Emma's vacant seat to get a closer look.

"Magnificent bit of engineering," said Kendal, showing off the real one ostentatiously dripping from his wrist.

"What's so good about them?" asked Bella.

Kendal clicked open the clasp and passed it along. She took the watch, her arm dropping a touch when its heft took her by surprise.

"It's powered by your wrist movement," Kendal explained proudly.

"No batteries?"

He nodded.

"You must save a fortune," Bella joked, passing it back.

"And when you go deep sea diving, no need to take it off," Charlie said. "That must come in very handy."

Kendal pulled out the winding crown and dialled the hour hand to reflect central European time.

"I wonder if we'll make the slopes this afternoon?" said Bella.

"Not at this rate. By the time we make it up to the resort, the lifts will be closed for the day," said Charlie.

Kendal shook his head, sadly. "Helicopter?" he suggested, only half joking.

Bella leaned across the aisle to the boys.

"Kendal, where's the birthday girl? They've finished loading the bags."

He looked at his phone, then sucked through his teeth.

"No messages from her," he said. "She insisted on visiting her father yesterday, and then decided to come straight to the airport. I told her she'd be late. So it goes."

"We are just waiting for one more passenger, and we'll be getting on our way," came a voice over the intercom. Several people groaned and looked at their watches.

"I think I can see her," Charlie said. "You didn't tell me she was injured."

Kendal leaned across his companions and raised his sunglasses onto his slicked-back golden hair. He peered through the porthole window and watched Emma being helped up the steps by a member of the cabin crew. She moved with a wooden, clunking motion as if she were a hundred years old. The air hostess ascended behind her, carrying what looked like a bird cage.

"Poor thing. She must have taken a fall," said Bella.

Emma appeared at the entrance of the plane and the air hostess passed her a long, wooden sledge. Emma nodded gratefully, gripping the curved runners like the handles of walking sticks. Chatter on the plane hushed and she self-consciously inched down the aisle.

"Are you sure she's going to be able to ski?" said Charlie. "She needs a zimmer frame to get down the plane."

Bella elbowed him.

As Emma reached the rear of the aircraft, Kendal got up to enable her to step into her seat, his face also fixed on the floor. She thanked the air hostess for stowing the sledge, and slid down into her seat until she all but disappeared. The door hissed shut, air shot from the overhead vents and the safety announcements began. Finally, the world's attention moved on.

"Are you okay?" Kendal asked.

She lifted up to check no staff were in earshot, then whispered so quietly that Charlie and Bella had to lean in to hear.

"I was late," she began.

"I told you not to go to your dad's," Kendal muttered.

"When I got to check in, I had two items, the sledge and my case. I checked in my case at the machine, but took my sledge as carry on."

"Did you check it fits into the frame?" said Kendal.

"No, I did not," she said. "Okay? I should have checked. I didn't check."

"You should have checked in with me. I would have got you to check."

"Kendal, let her speak," Bella said.

Emma stopped talking as a flight attendant paced up the aisle, flicking her head this way and that to check lap belts were in place. The plane began to taxi across the runway.

"So, at what point did you get arthritis?" Charlie asked.

"By the time I got to the lounge, the flight had boarded. I showed my ticket and was carrying this sledge. She took one look at it and said it's not coming on the plane. Won't fit on the overhead locker, blah, blah, blah."

"Couldn't you check it in?" Kendal asked.

"No, because the flight was about to take off, and anyway I'm not checking it in. It's too precious," she said.

"It's a sledge."

"It's my sledge. It's important," she said.

The conversation was paused by the noise of the engines firing up. Emma watched the suburbs of west London disappear beneath the clouds.

Bella leaned across. "Then what?" she said.

Emma once again checked she was out of earshot of the cabin crew.

"The woman at the gate looked at a bin, as if my only option was to discard it like a bottle of water. I told her it was a mobility aid."

Charlie laughed.

"Naturally, she was incredulous," Emma continued.

"Rightfully so," added Kendal.

"Whose side are you on?" she said. "Anyway, there was no choice but to do a demonstration, so I began using it like a walker. The Swiss Air lady rolled her eyes but allowed me on. Once outside, I had to continue walking slowly because I wasn't sure if she was looking out of the window."

Charlie and Bella were in stitches.

"I think it's brilliant," said Bella. "Are you going to do the charade all over again at Zurich, or just shake out your limp like you have been cured?"

Kendal flipped through the seatback magazine, clearly mortified at the prospect of having to watch Emma stagger down the aisle again. Emma sensed a coldness in the air.

"Thanks for bringing my case," she said.

He looked at her blankly, then gasped.

"Oh gosh. You're going to kill me," he said.

"Very funny," she responded.

The group were silent, staring at Kendal and hoping it was a joke.

"I'm sorry, Em, but I had so much going on this morning. I had to get the labels off my new jacket and dig out my passport. It just slipped my mind."

Emma's lips and eyes narrowed simultaneously, as anger built inside her.

"You aren't joking?" she said, holding back tears. "That bag had my laptop and underwear. It was like, the absolute minimum I could take for a week away."

Charlie held a horrified Bella, as if to reassure her that it wasn't *all* men she should hate, just that one man sitting a few seats over.

"I'm sorry, Emma, but you can't just swan off to the countryside and send me a text and expect me to do this all without you."

"All what? Putting my laptop and undies into your case?" she said.

"It's not just that though, is it? I had my new ski socks. My hand luggage. It's a lot to remember. I had to lock up the flat, and ... I nearly forgot my e-reader."

Charlie swallowed down a laugh as Kendal's to-do list fizzled out. With no kids to look after, no pets to feed, and a concierge that carried his luggage down to a waiting taxi, it was hard to reimagine Kendal's morning as an overwhelming routine. A tear ran down Emma's cheek, which she wiped away with her new jumper. The soft wool reminded her of her dad, and she kept it there a second, smelling the earthy freshness of the countryside. A frosty silence swept across the seat row.

"I'll buy you new stuff," Kendal said, patting her thigh, which she edged away. "Let's not let it ruin our holiday."

"Kendal, where am I going to buy bras in a Swiss ski village? My laptop is in that case. The charger."

At the mention of bras, Kendal raised his eyebrows and looked out of the window. He muttered something about not needing the charger if she didn't have a laptop, which Emma had to pretend not to hear. A flight attendant passed by with a trolley of refreshments.

"Can I get you anything?" he asked.

"Yes. A new boyfriend," Emma smiled.

"Well, I'm afraid you might be out of luck with my crew. But perhaps a gin and tonic would hit the spot?"

She stuck a thumb up, and he used tongs to transfer a couple of ice cubes into a plastic glass.

"At the end of the flight, you can disembark first. I'll bring your walker," he said.

"Oh," she said. "Right."

Bella squeaked in amusement.

"Better make that a double," Emma said.

"Right you are," he said, snapping open a can of tonic. "That'll be eighteen euros."

Chapter Four

The girls sat in the back row of the minivan that ferried the group to the resort. By the time they reached the foot of the valley, a plan had been formed to furnish Emma with some of Bella's spare clothes, at least until they could hit the shops. The driver slid open the door and the group stepped onto the icy car park of the train station.

"Cable car the rest of the way," Kendal announced. "No cars in the resort."

He held out a hand to help Emma dismount the minibus.

"Sorry, about your luggage," he said.

"It's okay. Bella is lending me some underwear. The shops will be shut when we arrive," she said.

He smiled mischievously and the girls shook their heads.

"I haven't seen that jumper before," Kendal said, changing the subject. "I sort of want to ask if it's new, but it looks, well...did you find a charity shop at the airport?"

"My dad made it," Emma said defiantly.

"Made it?" Charlie said, pinching the wool.

"Yes, he's quite the renaissance man, my dad."

"Can he make me one?" Bella said. "It looks cosy."

Kendal smirked. "I can find you a new jumper, darling, don't worry," he added.

The group dragged their luggage, or in Emma's case, carried her sledge and a carry-on bag, into the station.

"Did he make that sledge, too?" Charlie asked.

"I expect so. We've had it since we were kids," Emma replied.

"Certainly looks homemade," Kendal muttered as he collected tickets for a train which ran up the steep mountainside to their ski resort.

"Did your dad make things?" Bella nudged Charlie.

"He made money?" Charlie said, raising the inflection at the end to ask if that qualified. "Bella, remember that I saw my dad about three times a year. It was quite the event, like meeting the Prime Minister or the Queen. My mum would make sure I had a pressed shirt and knock respectfully on his study door. He'd ask serious questions about my academic milestones and sporting achievements."

"And he never presented you with a hand knitted jumper?" she said.

"Sadly not. But on my sixteenth he did give me an antique shotgun. So, there's that."

Alongside the train were deep, pillowy snowfields and then forests, dark foreboding combs of razor straight spruce. Beyond the trees, mountains cut a jagged silhouette against the purple washed sky.

"It's beautiful," Emma said, transfixed by the view.

Kendal put his arm around her, and she squeezed his hand. At the resort, the doors glided open smoothly and they lifted their cases from the train. Charlie, Bella, and Emma looked to Kendal, who thumbed around a map on his phone to find their chalet.

"This way," he announced, setting off down a winding side street. The little wheels of their suitcases cut trenches in the snow-covered pavement. Emma balanced her carry-on luggage onto the toboggan and towed it by a leather strap.

"I want one," Bella cried. "Charlie, buy me a zimmer frame!"

"There must be a shop where you can buy a laptop," Kendal said.

Emma flopped back on the bed, her phone resting limp on her hand.

"I searched 'Apple Store near me' and Google practically laughed. We're in the middle of nowhere. Even if I get the train to Zurich and buy a laptop, I would have to get the IT department to install some Fort Knox software to enable me to access the company files."

"Get the contracts faxed?" Kendal suggested.

"Faxed?" Emma said, sitting up. "Or perhaps a carrier pigeon? Just because we're lawyers, doesn't mean we're trapped in time."

Kendal pinched his fingers until they almost touched, and with his one open eye, looked at her through the gap. She whacked him with a pillow.

"Just tell him to stuff it," Kendal said. "Your boss is so needy. I told them you were on holiday. Blame me."

"About that," Emma said. "He seemed completely unaware. Are you sure you told Anthony?"

Kendal thumbed through his phone, then tossed it onto the bed. Emma saw that Kendal had used Facebook to contact Anthony and read his message aloud.

"'*Whisking Emma off to the mountains. Back to work a week Tuesday*'. To which Anthony replied, '*Aye aye, captain*', with a mountain emoji."

Kendal gave a self-satisfied, tight-lipped smile.

"And who is Anthony Davis?" she said, hiding her head in the crook of her elbow, face down on the bed.

Kendal snatched the phone back, tapping on the guy's profile.

"Oh. I see what happened now. That's kind of funny," he said, suppressing a chuckle.

"Is it?" Emma replied. "You just contacted the first Anthony you found and hoped for the best! Who is he?"

"Guy from school. Bloody good rower."

There was a gentle knock on the door of their bedroom, and Emma opened it to find Bella in a sumptuous white bathrobe. She stuck out a small stack of clothes which Emma took gratefully. A plain grey t-shirt, a plain black bra, two sets of socks and underwear.

"Are you sure?" Emma said, flushed with emotion.

"Of course. No need to give it back. I'll get more."

"Send Charlie shopping," Kendal interjected.

"No chance. If I send Charlie shopping for underwear, let's just say it'll come in a box with a ribbon."

Kendal raised his eyebrows. "My type of man," he said, with a pointed glance at Emma.

Bella had done her share of modelling in the dying days of lad mags. She even made the cover of *Stuff Magazine*, with a python coiled around her shoulders and an Apple gadget in her hand. As she hit her twenties, she transitioned to less lucrative but more stable work in the city, where she met Charlie. The framed image of her and the snake hung proudly for a time in their downstairs bathroom, but subsequently got relegated to the garage. Now the image of Bella seductively watches over a Lycra-clad Charlie as he wheels his carbon fibre bicycle into the driveway.

"Charlie and I are going into the hot tub," Bella said.

"I'll join you," Kendal said.

"Oh. Have fun," Emma said. "I don't have a cossie. I'll try to get one tomorrow."

Bella left, and Kendal rooted through his suitcase for swimming shorts. Emma held up Bella's huge bra to her chest.

"Don't think this is going to work," she said.

"Works for me," Kendal replied.

Emma swung it at his head, but he dodged, laughing.

"Would you ever consider..." he began, cautiously.

Emma gave him a sharp glance,

"Why, do you prefer Bella's?"

"No, of course not. But Bella seems happy. You should ask her which surgeon she used."

Not wanting another fight so soon after the laptop debacle, Emma just smiled tightly.

"I'm heading downstairs." Kendal announced, tossing a towel over his shoulder. "You can join me when you're done sulking about your clothes."

The chalet had started life as a farm building nearly two hundred years ago and had been renovated with no expense spared. The main room was double height, with exposed oak beams supporting a mezzanine that was once a hay loft. Leather sofas marked out a lounge, centred around a log burner which hung all the way from the roof like a black flying saucer.

Emma turned to enter the kitchen, distracted by the incessant vibrations coming from her phone.

She almost tripped over a person crouching by the oven, and both of them clutched their heart for a moment.

"I was in another world, sorry," said the chalet host. She opened the oven door and waved away a little smoke. A tray of vol-au-vents - crisp but not quite burned - were placed onto a trivet on the granite worktop.

She had pale skin with freckled cheeks, blushed red from the sun or the oven; Emma wasn't sure which. Messy blond hair fell across her face, and she blew it aside with fleshy lips, revealing a gap between her front teeth. Used to the sharp, manicured aesthetic of the city professional, Emma was struck by the wild, youthful beauty of the girl in the kitchen.

"I'm Alice," she said finally, pulling off her oven glove. "I'm your host." She extended her hand toward Emma.

"Nice to meet you, Alice. I didn't know we had a host."

"I do breakfast, cakes, and tea at about four, and dinner," Alice said.

"Fantastic. I'm Emma. I'm the greedy, insatiable one, who will gratefully out eat both of the boys at breakfast, tea, and dinner."

"Help yourself," said Alice. "I can cook more if we need them. Let me get you a drink."

Emma sat on a wooden stool with a cow hide seat and sipped a cold glass of pinot. Alice methodically worked through a to-do list, cleaning up constantly as she went.

"You look like you've done this before," Emma said.

"It's my fourth season," Alice replied. "Lasagne is the easiest night if I'm honest. Sling it in the oven. I mean, it's nice, an' all. Don't worry."

Emma laughed.

"I bet it is. So do you stay in the chalet, Alice?"

"Nah, this chalet is too small to need a full-time host, so I stay in staff accommodation up the road. I look after you and the one across the street. They're only bed and breakfast, though, so you'll get my full attention."

Emma went to the fridge and pulled it open. Alice hurried over.

"I can get that for you. You shouldn't be lifting a finger," she said.

Alice took the wine from Emma's hand and topped her up. Kendal's laugh was so loud it made it from the hot tub through the chalet's triple-glazed windows. Emma looked at Bella, who sat on the lip of the tub with her legs kicking gently at the water. Their eyes met, and Bella smiled, offering a little wave.

She slipped down into the water, lifting her hair to ensure it kept out of the water.

"You should join them," Alice said. "Weather is on the turn."

"Oh, really?" Emma said.

"Yep. A storm is inbound. Sorry, we're told to stay positive. I should say that there's some great skiing on the way."

"Join me for a drink," Emma said. "After all, you only have to sling a lasagne in the oven."

"Oh, go on then," Alice said, requiring very little convincing.

She reached for a delicate wine glass and poured herself a large pinot.

Alice deftly prepared a salad, while Emma repeatedly offered to help.

"We don't normally get to this stage til the end of the week," Alice said.

"What's that?"

"Drinking with the guests. I really shouldn't, but life's too short. So tell me, what do they do?" Alice asked.

"They?"

"The guys," Alice said.

"We all work in the city. I work in law; they work in banking."

Alice looked outside at Bella and sniggered.

"She doesn't work in banking," she said, refilling both of their drinks.

"What do you mean by that?" Emma asked.

"Look at her!" said Alice.

Out in the steaming hot tub, Bella noticed Alice and Emma looking at her through the window. In a moment of self-consciousness, she put her palms up as if to say 'what?' Alice lifted a bottle of wine from the fridge and pointed to it. Bella nodded eagerly, and Alice took a fresh bottle outside, screwing it into an ice mound by the side of the hot tub.

"No glasses in the hot tub, okay?" she said with a wink.

Kendal dutifully put his fingertips to his temple and saluted. Alice returned inside, shaking the snow from her boots as she slid the door shut.

"Yeah, she's not a banker. Sorry," Alice repeated.

"But I pass for a lawyer?" Emma said, not entirely sure how to take the assertion.

Alice flipped down the oven door and slid a heavy lasagne onto the wire shelf.

"Nah, I didn't mean like that. You are real pretty, Emma. You're both beautiful. I can just tell."

"You're too quick to judge," Emma said.

"But am I right?"

"Well, Bella used to work in banking, so not really. She worked with Charlie - that's the guy with shorter hair. But she doesn't work anymore."

"What did she do?" Alice pried.

"She was his personal assistant. There's a lot more to that role than..."

Too late. Alice sniggered victoriously. She stared wistfully out of the window, watching the three of them soak in the warm, bubbling water.

"That's what I need," she said, with a tea towel over her shoulder. "Someone to whisk me around the world, feed me olives and let me ski all day."

"You seem like a capable woman," Emma said. "You don't need a man to take you skiing. In fact, I bet you ski more days per year than they'll ski in a decade."

Alice appeared unconvinced. She topped up Emma and muttered "None for me, or I'll start dropping plates", but then filled her glass to the brim and stared longingly out of the window.

Chapter Five

"C an't we send someone?" Kendal whined. "The chalet girl, what's her name? She'll do it if we bung her a few quid."

Charlie patted his old school friend on the shoulder.

"Firstly, Kendal old chap, she's done for the day. Secondly, you can only send someone to fetch your ski boots if you chop your feet off so they can make sure they fit."

Kendal finished his beer and peeled himself off the sumptuous leather sofa.

"Alright, alright. Not worth a double amputation. Let's go."

The group threw on their coats and hats for the brief walk to the ski rental shop. They didn't lock the door, confident that this idyllic corner of Switzerland would be crime free.

Snow fell in gorgeous, huge flakes that left no trace when they brushed them from their shoulders. Emma took Kendal's hand as they kicked through the snow.

"How's the chalet girl?" Kendal asked. "You were talking to her for ages. I don't know what you say to these people."

"She's funny," Emma said. "How was the hot tub?"

"Wonderful. I was saying to Charlie, I'm thinking of getting one."

"A hot tub?" Emma asked.

"No, a chalet. It's a faff, renting equipment. Would be much more convenient if they were there, in the cupboard."

A bell rang, light and Christmassy, and Emma spun around to see a horse drawn sleigh approaching. The foursome moved aside to let it pass and its driver, bearded and draped in furs, doffed his cap. The street was lined with cosy-looking shops, some selling cheese and meats, and others with postcards and carved wooden ornaments. It was a picture-perfect mountain town.

"Yes, Kendal," Emma said. "This walk is quite hellish. We must avoid it next time, even if it costs a bazillion pounds."

He whacked her with his glove, and she giggled. The group soon arrived at a shop with empty racks outside. A man sat on a bench, staring at the floor between his boots. The fur of his parka obscured his face. Emma walked straight past him, assuming he was homeless or drunk, or both. She kicked her heels together like Dorothy from the Wizard of Oz, leaving a neat little ridge of snow on the rubber mat.

The interior of the ski shop took her back to the changing rooms at her secondary school. Whilst her brother was playing sensible sports like football at the local comprehensive, Emma had been packed off to an all-girls school where she found herself grappling with lacrosse sticks. The store had wooden benches along the sides, a bank of cubby holes populated with trainers and boots, and stacks of plastic toboggans. A shop counter straddled the middle of the room, and beyond it were racks and racks of colourful plastic ski boots and poles. Everything they could need was there, except someone to help them.

"Hellooo," Emma called.

The friends sat on a bench and took off their shoes in anticipation of being fitted. Kendal looked around impatiently, and after a few minutes, stepped outside.

"Excuse me, do you know when the owner will be back?" he asked the guy on the bench outside.

"I am him," he said, his face remaining in the shadow of his hood.

"Ah, rightyo. We've been waiting inside for some time. We're here to get fitted, so..." Kendal held the door open, extending his fingers to provide an arch through which the owner might step. But he didn't budge, choosing instead to remain in the falling snow.

"Please," the shop owner said. "Go inside and choose your boots. They are in the racks according to size."

Kendal returned into the warmth of the building, the bell making a 'ding' as the door swung shut.

"He *is* the owner, and he said just go for it," he announced, shaking his head.

"Why?" Emma said.

Kendal shrugged and stepped behind the counter to examine the library of ski boots. He picked out his size and carried them into the main part of the store.

Emma poked her head out of the shop door, unable to believe Kendal's report.

"Just to confirm; we help ourselves to ski boots," she said.

The man, face down, nodded. Emma returned to the store and selected some boots, as her boyfriend had done. Charlie and Bella did the same.

"Bet he gets off his arse to take our money," Kendal said, stamping his heel into a huge black plastic boot. He cranked the buckles shut and leaned forward so his weight was supported by his shins, and his heels lifted slightly from the ground. He noticed Emma was struggling to get hers on and held her hand so she could balance. She dropped suddenly as her heel slipped down into the boot.

Emma began to hobble around and said "I feel like a robot. Completely trapped. It's horrible."

"Perfect," said Kendal. "Welcome to skiing."

"But shouldn't I be able to wiggle my toes?" she said.

"Don't worry," Bella added. "Once you get up the mountain, they go numb anyway."

"Well, that's something to look forward to," Emma said. She walked around the shop with the grace of a staggering drunk.

"I think they fit," she said. "But are you sure I can't just go sledging? I'm really good. I did a jump once."

The others shook their heads in unison. Charlie poked his head out of the door.

"Skis. Help ourselves?" he said.

The man on the bench nodded, and Charlie laughed out loud.

"Help yourself," he relayed to the others. "It's self-service."

Kendal found the longest pair in the store and slapped them onto the carpet. He instinctively snapped to his sultry modelling face as he sported an aerodynamic crouch.

"How do I know which ones to get?" Emma asked.

"Get short ones," Bella said. "Up to your nose. They're easier to turn."

"I get the longest ones I can find," Kendal said proudly. "More stable. Short ones flap about like a couple of fish."

Emma stepped outside.

"We're trying to choose skis. Can you please help?" she said, irritably.

He stood up and pulled his hood back so he could see her properly, and Emma got a look at his face for the first time. He had a dark tan and crisp goggle marks, with a shadow of stubble around his jawline.

"174 centimetres?" he said, looking her up and down.

"Fine," she replied, heading back into the shop.

"No, no, come back," he said.

She turned back, hands on hips. "Not the skis. You. I guess one hundred and seventy-four centimetres."

"Me? I'm not sure in centimetres. I'm five foot eight."

He pondered for a moment.

"173 centimetres," he said, emphasising the three to show off how close his guess was. "Beginner?"

"No, that was a very good guess. I'd say you're intermediate," Emma said.

"I mean you. Skiing. Are you a beg..."

"I know, I know. Yes, I'm a beginner."

He smiled as her joke sank in. She hadn't thought it possible his moody demeanour could crack until now.

"Okay, you need 160-centimetre skis. Please bring them out with your boots and I will fit the bindings."

She nodded and returned through the door. As she crossed the threshold, she leaned her head back out into the snow.

"You know, you could come inside and do it here? There's a roof. It's very effective."

He shook his head, and Emma shrugged.

One by one, the group took their gear outside and handed them to the shop owner. He crouched on the snowy pavement in the dim light of his own shop windows, holding a small torch between his teeth. He snapped their boots into their bindings and made the necessary adjustments, depending on his estimates of their heights and weight.

When he had completed Bella's, he nodded, his face slipping back into the shadow of his parka hood.

"We pay when return?" Kendal asked. Emma chuckled under her breath at his pidgin English, as if they were in Papua New Guinea. The store owner shrugged and reached an arm into his own shop to turn off the lights.

The English party trudged off in the snow, looking back to see the strange man locking up his store.

"So, am I a skier now?" Emma asked.

"Well, not yet. You haven't actually skied," said Bella.

Emma propped her equipment against a building and bit the fingertip of her mitten to pull it from her hand. She fumbled in her pocket for her phone and passed it to Bella.

"Can you take a pic? Before I break my leg."

Kendal reached an arm around his girlfriend and flashed a pose for the camera. He had a well-rehearsed photo face in which he cocked his head down and to the side, lips tight shut with the slightest hint of a smile. He exuded confidence and poise, but never looked as though he was having fun. Emma, meanwhile, tended to overcompensate, and in photos she ended up looking like the parent of an embarrassed teenager.

Emma immediately sent it to her mum with the caption, '*In Switzerland. Thinking of the day at Barrow's Hill*'.

Back at the chalet they stashed their belongings in the boot room in the basement. Kendal brushed the snow from his jeans and stored his ski boots on a rack which gently circulated air to dry out clothes. He tried, unsuccessfully, to not gawp at Bella as she removed her jacket and salopettes.

"I'll go and grab some jeans upstairs," she said, self-consciously.

"Why am I totally unsurprised that even in thermal underwear you look like a movie star?" Emma said.

"Aww, thanks Em."

"So, what time are we going skiing in the morning?" Emma asked as they made their way up the wooden steps to the main level.

"Well, *we* were planning to go up the cable car at eight or nine," Kendal said. "But I don't think the slope we're taking is suitable for beginners."

"You did book lessons for Emma, didn't you?" Bella asked.

There was a pregnant pause as the three of them waited for Kendal to answer.

"I had a lot to do before we left..." He began, and everyone sighed.

"It's a little trickier than sledging," Charlie said. Bella whacked him.

"Lessons? Oh, right. Of course," Emma said. She looked embarrassed as she typed 'ski lessons near me' into her phone.

"Kendal said that skiing was like riding a bike. Which I'm pretty good at. I sort of took that too literally."

"Indeed, they don't have handlebars and brakes," Charlie said.

"Yeah, yeah. I got that much. I'll just get an instructor and learn fast, then I can come skiing with you later in the week," Emma said.

They nodded unconvincingly, and the evening passed quietly with chatting around the log fire, while Emma searched endlessly for a ski instructor.

"They're all booked up," she said. "All the online sites have nothing available this week. This really might be as far as I get as a skier," she joked, showing them the photo of her and Kendal, grinning outside the rental store.

"Hey, pass me that phone, Em," Bella said, sitting up.

She did so, and Bella zoomed in on the photo.

"There's a phone number on the storefront which says Lessons. Worth a shot?"

Bella passed the phone back, and Emma typed out a message. *'Do you have any lessons available... tomorrow?'*

There was no response, and she set her phone down on the table. She sighed and took her wine glass to the sink where she poured the last of it down the plughole.

"Shall I just come up on the cable car with you guys and go for it?" Emma said.

"Kendal can teach you," Bella suggested. "He should have booked lessons when he booked the holiday."

Emma looked at her partner, who looked crestfallen.

"I'm just not sure I'm qualified," he said. "I learned twenty years ago. And it's not going to be any fun for Emma; you know I'm terrible at teaching things."

"It's fine. I'll figure something out," Emma said. "It's just nice to be here. In the morning, I'll go into town and see if I can find a lesson to tag along with."

Her phone pinged.

"Yes!" she said. "I have a ski instructor. 9am at the lifts."

"Great," Kendal said. "If that doesn't work out, I'm really happy to teach you, babe. So, see how you get on, and just know that I'm available if you need me."

"Thanks Kendal," Emma said.

Bella and Charlie turned in for the night, leaving Kendal and Emma at each end of the couch.

"Shall we go upstairs too?" Emma said.

"I was thinking of getting another drink," Kendal said.

Emma raised her eyebrows.

"Are you sure?" she said. "I do have some undersized boobs you can play with?"

He smiled, then went to the fridge freezer and dispensed some ice cubes. She knelt on the sofa and looked over the back of it.

"Kendal, we've been together for two years. Why does it sometimes feel like twenty?" she said.

"What do you mean?" he said, pouring a whisky.

"You know what I mean. We used to be at it like rabbits."

He gently bit his bottom lip, and returned to the lounge, kissing her on the forehead.

"It's just work," he said. "I'll unwind here."

They sat side by side on the sofa, looking into the flickering log fire. They put their feet up, and Kendal opened a brochure of properties. Emma placed her hand on his thigh and gave it a playful squeeze, then crawled it towards his crotch. He put his hand onto hers, stopping the spider in its tracks.

"Why aren't you into getting a chalet?" he said.

"I didn't say that," she replied.

He flipped the magazine shut and sipped his drink. She rested her head on his shoulder.

"This place is amazing, Kendal. The crackle of logs on the fire, ice cold wine, squirty soap dispensers. I just don't necessarily need to own the whole building. That's okay, isn't it?"

"Of course. It's just..." he began.

She raised her head from his shoulder and looked at him.

"Well, most girls," he continued, before adjusting his opening. "Most people, partners ... would be impressed. Blown away by the idea of owning a place like this," he said, motioning at the gorgeous interior.

She nodded.

"I guess I'm not most girls," she said.

"No, I guess not."

"You have to remember, Kendal, that my childhood was about sleeping out in a den, taking a Thermos of hot chocolate to the beach, trying to summon ghosts in a barn... But don't get me wrong, I am blown away that you brought me skiing for my birthday. I'm not ungrateful. I love the adventure. I'm just not fussed about owning expensive things."

He raised his eyebrows.

"And I am?" he said, defensively.

She dragged up his shirt cuff to reveal a twenty-thousand-pound Rolex Daytona. She toed the picture of the ski chalet he had been salivating over in the magazine, and then pinched her fingers together, looking at him through the tiny gap.

"A little," she said.

Chapter Six

♥

Emma gnawed at a loop of string that linked a cardboard tag to her brand new salopettes. As the fibres became fine, she tugged it apart and stuffed it into a zip pocket, grateful to never have to see that price again. She eagerly replaced her mittens and picked up her cup from the snow. With the smell of fresh coffee and the sound of children playing, she closed her eyes and exhaled happily, her breath misting in the air.

She reread the text message from her ski instructor, which simply said, 'Meet by the lifts at 8:30'.

Emma looked around the snowy expanse that marked the intersection between the town and the slopes. Ski boots were being buckled shut, sun cream being smeared onto cheeks, and tracker apps were being launched. Three lifts radiated out from this starting point, scooping up skiers six to a bench, and whisking them high into the clouds. There was also a gondola, which looked like a series of goldfish bowls hanging on a wire. Instructors tapped their ski poles above their heads, and groups of sleepy children in oversized crash helmets snaked after them obediently.

Emma stood roughly in the middle of the area, unsure whether she was part of a lift queue or not. She put her skis down and, as Bella had taught her, poked the plastic toe cap of her boot into a binding, then stamped her heel onto the backplate. It clunked satisfyingly shut, and she did the other one. She sank into a racing pose, almost toppling to the side, when her phone beeped.

'*Where are you?*' a message said.

She tapped a reply.

'*Near the Honegg lift. Brown hair. Coral hat.*'

Without her mittens on, her fingers were stung by the cold morning air. She stared impatiently at the screen, blowing warm air into her cupped palms. She looked around her, identifying a group of Germans huddled around a piste map and a fabulous looking woman in a leopard print all-in-one ski suit. But no ski instructor.

'*Coral?*' came a text.

"*How did it take him three minutes to write five letters?*" she thought to herself.

'*Kind of pinky-orange,*' she wrote back.

She attempted to turn around, but the skis were cumbersome, and she was stuck. Bella's lesson had not got as far as how to remove them.

'*Pinky?*' he replied, at last.

An exasperated Emma began to tap her ski poles above her head like the local professionals. A hand tapped her shoulder and she turned so suddenly that she fell in a twisted heap. Her skis stuck out of the snow like logs on a campfire. A man in a wheat-coloured parka held out a hand, which she batted away.

Emma attempted to untangle herself, only to fall back onto her bum. She sat on the snow and looked up at the ski instructor, who once again extended a hand. She accepted it and he hoisted her back to her feet. As she drew close, she recognised the chiselled jaw and tanned face of the oddball from the ski rental.

"Oh, it's you," she said, with crushing disappointment.

He looked around, slightly confused.

"From the ski shop. We met last night," Emma said.

He nodded.

"I am Leon," he said. "You must be Emma."

Emma dusted the snow from her bum. Leon set down his skis and clipped his boots in.

"Well, I don't need to tell you how to put your skis on. You already did it," he said. "So, let's go."

"Shouldn't you teach me how to take them off?" Emma asked.

He began to needle his way into a crowd which got denser as it neared the chairlift.

"No need. Your skis will come off automatically when you crash. And at lunch time. Not yet," he called back.

"But I don't want to crash," Emma said.

She shuffled after him, using her poles to steady herself. They worked their way to a roped off gangway marked 'ski school', which provided a fast track to the turnstiles. Leon glanced over his shoulder to make sure Emma had kept up, and raised his forearm to one of the barriers. It beeped, flashed green and the turnstile let him through. Emma slid toward it and raised her arm as he had done. Nothing.

"Push it right against the barrier," Leon said.

She did so, but the barrier remained resolutely closed. Leon kicked the back of his binding and unclipped, walking back to his student. He lifted her arm, inspecting her jacket for a zip.

"There's no pocket here," he said. "Where's your pass?"

"What pass?" she said.

"Then what were you trying to beep?" he said. Her blank look told him the answer.

A line of children had formed behind Emma, and she scooted aside to let them through. Checking the lift operator was pre-occupied, Leon reached back and beeped his own pass against the sensor for a second time. The turnstile spun forward and he pulled Emma through. She found herself on a plastic conveyor belt which lurched her and Leon forward. Emma shrieked when she saw that the moving black road was about to waterfall into an orange net.

"Get ready to sit," he said.

"On what?" Emma replied, looking back just as a six-person bench materialised out of thin air and swung into the backs of her knees. In the shock of the moment, she remained frozen, surging toward the abyss. Leon pressed a hand on her stomach and she folded back into the seat. The nervous-looking liftie removed his hand from the panic button as the couple were hoisted into the air.

Leon lowered the bar slowly, sensing that she wouldn't appreciate any more surprises. He lifted his skis and placed them onto a footrest. Emma did the same.

Her heart pounded and she looked down at the lift queue that was drifting quickly into the distance.

"Do we have to do that again?" she said.

"Eventually, yes," he said.

"You could have told me I would need a lift pass," she said.

He raised his forearm and pressed it against her shoulder, making a beep to imitate the barriers. He chuckled. She didn't.

"Doesn't matter now. Save your money. Once we get to the top, we can use the magic carpet."

The chairlift whirred gently as it ascended above the snowy tips of spruce and larch. Emma looked up at the sky, unable to face the fifty-foot drop beneath them. She gripped the bar every time their chair clunked past a tower.

"What do we do at the top?" she asked, nervously.

"We ski," he said.

"Yes, I know that. I mean, what happens at the top of the lift? I like to plan. I like to know what's happening," she said.

He looked at her with narrowed eyes, as if the very concept was alien.

"But surprises are fun," he said.

She shook her head. "I hate surprises."

"I bet you were fun at Christmas," he said.

"I was, actually. Am. But when I'm getting dragged onto ski lifts at nine in the morning, I feel shunted around like cattle."

He cocked his head to the side, giving his best confused look.

"Cattle? Like, cow," she said.

"What is 'cow'?" he replied.

They locked eyes, and the silence hung heavy and long in the still morning air. Finally, she moo'd. He chuckled.

"What's so funny?" she said.

"I know what a cow is," he said. "I'm Swiss. I just wanted to see if you would moo. Relax Emma. We will have fun."

She gave a snort of irritation, realising a second too late that it, too, sounded a little bovine.

Below their skis was a steep, forested incline with several trees snapped off at the base, leaving giant toothpicks jutting from snow. Leon pointed out a pine marten track, but Emma refused to look down. In any case, it was probably a stupid joke, or a trick. As they approached the top, the sun burst through a gap in the clouds, warming their faces instantly.

"So, when we reach the top, it will slow down," Leon said. "We'll take our feet off these pegs and I will lift up this bar. You will feel your skis gently connect with the snow. Then you stand up. Simple. The lift will push on the backs of your legs. Just stand up, and let the lift do the work."

"How do I stop?" she said. "What if I go all the way down the mountain?"

"You won't. Don't worry," he laughed, taking her poles from her.

The lift began to slow and Leon lifted his skis from the footrests. Once Emma had done the same, he raised the safety bar. She looked at him anxiously.

"Look forward," he said. "And keep those tips up."

She did so, bringing them so high that her skis slapped loudly on the snow when her tails met the offloading slope. Emma stood up, as instructed, and was pushed forward by the lift. She careened into a huddle of skiers planning their route, tearing their piste map as she scrambled for support.

"Hi," she said. "Sorry. I'm stuck."

The tourists politely extracted their skis from beneath Emma's, and she was once again hauled away by Leon. He towed her across the snowy plateau to a quiet spot, where she was finally able to breathe. She sat on the snow, buzzing with adrenaline and already exhausted.

"It's quite intense," she said.

He looked at her blankly.

"We haven't started yet. Now, Emma, you like pizza, right?"

She looked down at her tummy and sucked it in.

"As much as the next person. Everyone likes pizza, don't they?" she said.

He unclipped his bindings and jabbed his skis into the snow like tombstones. Crouching in front of Emma, he tugged her ski tips together. Before he touched her legs, he looked at her with raised eyebrows. She nodded, and he cupped the insides of her calves to nudge her boots apart. The breezy confidence with which he muscled her around took her by surprise. Here was a person with a job to do.

"You make a pizza slice, like this," he said.

Emma's ski tips touched, and her knees were shoulder width apart. He moved behind and pinched the backs of her skis, sliding them together and apart.

"Narrow pizza is fast, wide is slow. Got it?"

She nodded. "Sort of."

"Show me," he said, holding her hands.

With great concentration, Emma stepped her skis together and then pushed them wider and wider until her knees felt like they may buckle.

In this final position, Leon stepped behind and put his hands on her lower back, easing her onto the slope. She began to slide forward at walking pace and gritted her teeth. Snow built up against the outside edges of her skis and eventually forced them to narrow. As they did so, she picked up speed. Leon jogged alongside.

"Wide pizza!" he said.

"I can't!" she replied. "They just go straight."

Leon was running now to keep up, and Emma began to shriek. Ahead of them, the gentle green run came to an end with a queue for a lift. By the time they hit the halfway mark, Emma's skis were parallel and she was going so fast that Leon could barely keep up at a run.

"Help!" she gasped. The more she looked at the people in the lift queue, the more she seemed to steer towards it.

"Do a pizza!" Leon shouted, sprinting alongside her in his heavy ski boots.

"SHUT UP ABOUT PIZZA! she screamed. "I'm not FIVE!"

A lift technician darted out from his cabin and waved his arms above his head, shouting 'whoa' as if Emma were a horse. He placed himself as a human fence to protect the queue of beginners at his lift and spread his arms to catch her.

With a few metres to go before impact, Leon dived at Emma's legs and rugby tackled her into a snowbank. Her skis disconnected and the two of them tumbled into the soft powder. The crowd cheered, and Leon stood to take a bow, spitting out a mouthful of snow. Emma dusted herself off and forced a smile.

"Are you okay?" Leon asked, as he pulled her up.

"Just about," she said.

"Great. Let's go!" he said, skating off toward the lift queue they had nearly decimated.

Emma remained on the ground, digging through layers of sleeve and mitten to expose the face of her watch. She didn't know why, exactly. Perhaps to distract herself from the people staring at her from the lift. Perhaps wishing it was time for lunch, or the end of the day. Even better, time to return to London.

Skiing, she already knew, wasn't for her. It was cold and wet. It was embarrassing and painful. Worst of all it required spending time with an oaf who batted her around like a cat with a mouse. Precious time when she could be reading up on contracts and getting back in her boss's good books.

"Emma, you are a skier now," he said. "You never forget that first run."

"I can try," she muttered.

"This time, we will do the same, but try to control your speed and not straight line it towards the people queuing for the lift."

"Oh, I see," she said. "I couldn't remember if you said pizza slice or bowling ball. It's your accent."

"You're funny, Emma," he laughed.

The gentle beginner slope looked much steeper the second time around. Emma had become painfully aware how rapidly she could accelerate, and how powerless she was when it happened. She shuffled her skis into a V-shape. The tips scratched against each other.

Leon crouched behind her and lifted the backs of her skis, prising her legs even further apart.

"Can you give me some warning when you do that?" she said.

"This position is good," he said.

He nudged her forward, with his hands on her hips.

"Don't push me!" she said. "I want to go slowly."

Emma inched down the slope at a glacial pace, while Leon walked alongside, giving words of encouragement. She moved so slowly that he eventually jogged ahead and waited at the bottom. He sat in the snow and gave a genuinely excited clap when she finally arrived at the lift line.

"Very good, Emma. You did one run too fast. One too slow. So we must experiment with the angles of your skis to get a comfortable speed."

Emma nodded.

The magic carpet was a playful name for an airport travelator shrouded by a curved roof. It slowly transported skiers, almost all of them under seven, up the side of the beginner slope they had been practising on. Surrounded by little people who looked like colourful mushrooms with their bobbing crash helmets, Emma found the root of her irritation. She felt like a child. The pizza metaphor. The 'magic carpet'. Being saved by a big strong man. It grated on her.

She was never good at being a kid. Her parents joked that she was a lawyer in a nine-year-old's body, waiting for the world to take her seriously. Only her mum understood. But now Emma found herself sidelined to the creche while the grown-ups were off skiing. She thought of her colleagues, eagerly chomping through small-print while she was riding a magic carpet with two-year-olds who were already irritatingly competent skiers.

She realised Leon was talking to her, making motions with his hands to demonstrate angles of skis. Behind his head she saw the light at the end of the tunnel, and he continued to look into her eyes as the magic carpet spilled him out into the world.

"Emma, are you okay?" he said.

"No," she said, defiantly. "I'm getting lunch."

"Burger please. No bun. Salad instead of fries," Emma said, handing the menu to the waitress.

Leon shook his head, pulling a sandwich from his inside pocket and dumping it on the table. It was curved and flattened, its liquified filling smooshed against the clear plastic wrap. Another casualty of their crash, Emma presumed.

The server nodded and slipped the order pad into her apron.

Emma withdrew her phone and instinctively opened her email. She dragged down on the screen to refresh, but the animated arrow whirled around like a dog chasing its tail. She switched to her camera reel and flicked through images of the party, and her dad's farm. Leon rested his head on the wooden railing and let the rays soak into his skin.

Leon had already demolished his sandwich when the waitress brought Emma's meal, bun on the side. He gratefully took it, squirted a spiral of ketchup and gave it an artistic twist of pepper.

"The pepper really makes it," he said. "Are you enjoying skiing?"

"I don't know." She sighed, setting aside a pickle, which Leon promptly inserted into the burger bun. "It's beautiful here. I just feel like I'm a kid. On this baby slope, while all the adults whizz past. And 'pizza slice'. I'd prefer you talk to me like an adult."

"Sure. You seem uptight. You and your boyfriend, are you happy?" Leon said quite casually, crunching into his pickle sandwich.

Emma set down her knife and fork and cocked her head to the side.

"I'm sorry, what did you just say?"

He chewed a mouthful, reeling his index finger to indicate that she must wait a moment for his reply. He swallowed, and stood up next to their table, raising his hands to his armpits and pushing his elbows back. He crouched slightly, and vibrated, as if he were being electrocuted. Emma's shock at his question about her love life was now snowballing.

"You are like this," he said, shaking on the spot. "Tense."

Emma's jaw fell. Leon sat back and chomped on his pickle burger.

"That is highly inappropriate," she said.

He nodded, indifferently.

"And inaccurate," she added. "Anyway, if we're prying; why were you sitting in the cold outside your ski shop?"

He breathed in heavily.

"My employee was sick. Didn't show up for work. I had to lock up," he said.

"That's not what I asked," she persisted. Leon didn't respond.

Emma finished her salad while Leon reclined and looked out over the slopes, periodically whistling to friends who rocketed past.

"This afternoon," he said. "Let's get savage."

"Savage?"

He leaned in, wide eyed and a little psycho.

"Yes. You cannot learn to ski if you are tight like..."

He looked around the table for inspiration, and then once again moved his hands up to his chest so his elbows stuck out behind him. Emma rolled her eyes.

"Oh please, don't do the sexless velociraptor again," she said, under her breath.

He grinned and leaped off his seat once more. He thrusted his arms forward this time, and spread his fingers into a claw.

"This afternoon you are a T-REX! Gobble-up these slopes. Green. Blue. Red. Black!"

"...aaand I'm six years old again," Emma muttered.

Their waitress came by and shook her head gently.

"Calm down Leon, we have guests," she said. "Would you like coffee, dessert..? Not you, Leon. Caffeine and sugar are the last thing you need."

Emma nodded and Leon slunk back in his chair, resting his head on a wooden beam and squinting at the sun.

The waitress brought two coffees, to Leon's surprise.

"It's on the house. Bring me some eggs some time," she said.

"I will. I will," he said. "But it's cold, you know?"

She nodded, understanding. Emma asked for the bill.

Chapter Seven

"Anthony, I can't really speak now," Emma said. "I'm literally up a mountain."

She stood on a plateau outside a restaurant, with her hand covering her unused ear. Leon sat in one of the many deck chairs scattered on the snow, trying to tempt a finch to take crumbs from his open palm. A chairlift whirred and a steady stream of skiers passed by.

"Emma, he's on a warpath," Anthony said. "I'm going to have to put you through."

"He's always on a warpath," Emma said with a sigh.

"Warpath?" came the voice of her boss.

Emma cleared her throat.

"Hello, Nigel. We're on a warpath," she said. "To land this client. I was just discussing strategy with Anthony. Lead the attack, and all that."

"Right. Exactly," he said. "Where are you? I can't hear you very well."

"I've been looking through these documents all morning," she said loudly, ignoring Leon's raised eyebrows. "It's interesting stuff. The numbers they are dealing with are eye-watering."

"So, what have you got for me?" Nigel said.

"I need more time before I have any formal recommendations," she said.

A silence hung in the air.

"Nothing?" he said.

"Well, from what I've read so far, it doesn't look good. They were aware of the issue at least five years before they took any action."

"Emma, have you forgotten whose side you're on? We're not going to win a client by pointing out they've fucked up. They've got the whole bloody world doing that."

He exhaled so heavily that Emma could almost smell his dragon breath from five hundred miles away.

"I need more time," she said. "I'll work on it this afternoon."

"Don't bother," he said. "I'll have the others work on it."

The line went dead.

Emma pocketed her phone and sat next to Leon. She puffed out her cheeks and exhaled. Her right hand was white from holding the phone, and Leon placed his glove on top of it.

"You have problems with your work?" he said.

She nodded, snatching her hand away and stuffing it back into a mitten. Frustration simmered into anger, and Leon was the only person within firing range.

"The problem is, I'm stuck up a mountain when I should be in London. I've got no laptop because Kendal forgot it. I can't work on my phone. My boss just told me he's giving *my job* to someone else."

"That's good, right?" Leon said, hopefully.

She scowled.

"No, Leon, it's not good."

"You should turn off your phone. You're Fun Emma," he began, before bringing an imaginary mobile to his ear. "Then Mean Emma. Fun Emma. Mean Emma."

She scrunched her face in irritation. It was the sort of puerile attack she would have expected of her brother whilst waiting for the school bus. Not from a grown man she barely knew.

"With all due respect, I don't need career advice from a ski instructor."

"Ouch," he said, heaving himself out of the deck chair. "Classic Mean Emma. Anyway, my job isn't so bad. My office has a nice view."

Leon motioned to the stunning landscape that surrounded them, jagged mountains stretching for hundreds of miles in every direction. Emma felt a pang of bitterness for investing so much energy into getting an office overlooking a jungle of concrete. But her office was up high, and other people were below. And in London that meant she was winning.

"Well good for you. But we can't all teach people to ski," she said.

Leon offered out a hand to Emma, but she remained in the deck chair, arms folded across her chest.

"One hour," he said. "Just try to go one hour without your phone."

"You don't understand. My work is really busy, and they don't realise I'm on holiday. Which is a real pain because..."

"Your boyfriend forgot your laptop," Leon said. "And your boss is giving your work to someone else. I get it. Mean Emma told me already. Now let's ski. It will clear your mind. The world will continue just fine without you being connected to your office."

Her eyes widened.

"Well, that got existential," she muttered.

He pulled her up and they trudged through the snow to collect their skis.

"Leon, I don't mean to snap," Emma said. "Just having a bad day."

"Don't worry, me too," he said. "My client won't get off her phone."

As they queued for a drag lift, Emma got increasingly nervous. One by one, skiers ahead of her tucked a long metal pole between their thighs which hauled them up the slope. She shuffled forward, looking back for some advice from her instructor.

"All you have to do is relax," Leon assured her.

"Leon, I need tactics. A plan. When I want to *relax*, I watch a Christmas movie and eat trail mix. Should I do that? No."

He ushered her into the vacant launch spot, where she nervously threaded the aluminium pole between her thighs. She watched the complicated interplay of metal gears above her head and listened for the ominous clunk, still yelping with surprise when the drag lift yanked her forward.

"Relax!" Leon said.

Emma consciously untensed by summoning her inner couch potato, a character she rarely allowed out. For a moment she became Cameron Diaz's suitcase, dragged unceremoniously up a cobblestone pathway in The Holiday. Her thighs loosened and she let the button behind her bum take her weight. To her surprise, she found her skis obediently following the grooves left by other skiers, and she was able to breathe once more.

Going uphill, she discovered, was significantly less stressful than going down. Snow covered fir trees to her left, skiers swishing joyously down the slope to her right. With no risk of speeding out of control, she found herself comfortable enough to take her hands from the pole. Emma slipped off a glove and took her phone from her pocket, keeping it down by her hips and out of Leon's sight. She messaged her assistant, Anthony.

'Who has Nigel got working on the Swiss client?' she asked.

Her left ski bounced out of its track and her legs began to separate. "No, no, no," she said, as the ski drifted out into the undulating wilderness to the side of the lift run. As her thighs were pulled apart, the button popped out and shot out of her grasp. She collapsed in a heap, her phone skipping from her hand and landing alongside her in the snow.

Leon shook his head, releasing his button lift and letting it spring away from him.

"I relaxed too hard," she said.

He stooped over her and collected her phone from the snow. "What are you doing?" she said.

"I'm taking your phone," he replied. "You can't be trusted."

She let out a shriek of exasperation.

"Oh really, *Dad*? You're actually doing this?"

As he helped her to her feet, she swung an arm to retrieve her phone. He pulled it out of reach and slipped it into his chest pocket, tapping the flap for effect.

"We're here to ski, Emma. You can't be working and skiing. Anyway, you got fired, I think."

"I did not get fired!" she snapped. "If you had been listening, you would know he's giving the work to someone else."

"That's the same thing," Leon said. "Now come on, let's practise your snowplough. See? Snowplough, not pizza slice. I am listening."

Emma slid forward and snatched the flap of Leon's breast pocket. He smiled and pushed on his poles, slipping backwards into the slope.

"Nope. You want your phone, you must come and get it," he said.

"Are we twelve?" she asked.

Emma stabbed her poles into the snow to fight her way out of a flat spot. She began to slide down the piste, barely noticing that it was a steeper blue run than she had so far tackled. She picked up speed, then realising she was going too fast, instinctively slammed on the brakes by swinging her legs into a wide V-shape. It worked, and she smoothly ground to a halt.

"You got it!" Leon said, with a flash of white teeth. "When you're mad, you're really good."

He backed away from her, and Emma continued to follow him down the mountain. After an exhausting twenty minutes, they reached the end of the run, where it met the gondola station. Emma skidded to a stop; goggles steamed up from exertion.

She stared daggers at Leon and thrust her hand toward him, palm outstretched. He slapped her phone into it.

"We're done, Leon," she said. "I'm going down."

"One more run?" he said.

"School's over. I'm finished," she said, stamping on her bindings to eject her skis.

Emma slid the bases together and rested them on her shoulder. With heavy steps she trudged toward the lift that would take her back to town. Leon watched her walk away, shaking his head when she looked down at her phone.

The gondola station was a boxy building which echoed with the clunk of boots and the whirr of a gargantuan motor. Huge fish bowls hung from a cable, into which exhausted skiers filed in through sliding doors. The polite but aggressive scrum reminded Emma of her London commute, and the window steamed in front of her face.

At the thought of the city, she sank a little lower on her exhausted thighs, her weight pulling on a rubber strap above her head. She looked at her phone. No reply from Anthony. No missed calls. Leon was right. Nobody missed her at all.

She texted her mum.

'*Skiing is cold and wet and painful. Ski instructor a lunatic. Miss London. I think. Miss you.* x'

Her boss was prone to dramatic rhetoric. She would knuckle down when she got back to the chalet, think of something ingenious to say and send a midnight email. This could be fixed; all of it. She resolved to put Leon and this awful day behind her.

The lift doors opened and its colourful passengers spilled out onto criss-cross rubber matting. The gondola only slowed as people disembarked, and after a long day it gave Emma the dizzying sensation of stepping off a roundabout. She retrieved her skis and poles from the outside and set off toward the town square.

Leon was sitting on a wall, hood over his head and boots dangling. He spotted her and hopped down.

"Emma," he said.

She jumped.

"Oh lord, are you stalking me? How did you get here?"

"I skied. That's my job."

"Faster than that lift?" she said.

"Of course. I'm not you," he laughed. "Is it okay if you pay me now?"

"Oh. Sure. Can you text me your bank details? I think you allowed me my phone back," she said.

He nodded.

Emma scooped up her equipment, nearly decapitating a tourist as she swung a ski onto her shoulder. She joined the lazy river of tired skiers making their way toward town centre. Leon clunked noisily alongside her, saying hi to nearly everyone.

"Good day, ha?" he said.

She nodded, even forcing a polite smile despite her aching thighs and blistered shin.

He came to a halt and leaned his gear against the steamed up window of a bar. Emma continued trudging through the snow toward her chalet.

"You know how we end a wonderful day? Caspers!" he called after her.

She shook her head.

"I've had a wonderful day," she said, mostly to herself. "But this wasn't it."

Chapter Eight

E mma hung up her sodden clothes and painfully levered off the hard, plastic boots. The bridge of her foot was paper white and ice cold, with an angry red line where it had rubbed against the buckle. She wiggled her toes to bring some life back into them, quite relieved to find they still flexed. Through the ceiling of the basement she could hear music and the chit-chat of lazy banter from the others. She crawled up the stairs to the lounge like it was the final stage of Everest.

"You can do it, Emma," said Bella, leaning over the back of the sofa. "How was your first time skiing??"

"Well, I'm alive. But I need wine. And cheese. And a new ski instructor."

Emma crawled to the sofa area and drowned herself in the sumptuous leather, face down.

"What did he do to you?" Charlie asked with raised eyebrows. Bella whacked him.

"Eww," Emma said. "Remember the oddball from the ski shop who refused to come inside?"

"No!" Bella said, eyes wide.

"Yes! It's him, and he's infuriating. Dragged me around, pushed me over. He's a buffoon."

"Get a new one," Kendal said without looking up from his phone. "Buffoons are a dime a dozen in ski resorts."

"Well, it wasn't easy to find an instructor when I looked yesterday. But I am definitely going to try. If not, I will just ski on my own." Emma said, stretching her toes back and forth with a groan. "That hill feels very long in ski boots."

"You walked it? No, Em." Bella said gently, while Kendal laughed. "You're meant to leave them at the shop in town."

Emma curled into a ball and beat herself with a cushion.

"What's for dinner?" she asked, raising her head above the back of the couch to look for Alice. Kendal sucked through his teeth.

"The chalet girl is off tonight. She left us a casserole. It's her birthday, you see, so we said that was okay."

Emma peeled herself off the couch and walked to the kitchen, shaking some life into her limbs.

"Hey, shall I fetch your zimmer frame?" Charlie asked.

Emma shot him a curt glance. On the worktop was a casserole wrapped neatly in tin foil.

"Do you know how to use the oven?" Kendal asked. "It's just that we saw you in here with Alice last night, so hoped you would..."

His sentence tailed off.

"Sure. I'll cook. You wash up. How's that?" she said, rolling up the sleeves of her thermal top and twisting the knob on the oven.

Kendal laughed, and then stopped abruptly when he realised that the notion of him washing up wasn't a joke.

"We can wash up," Bella said, tapping Charlie on the thigh.

Emma deftly prepared a salad and poured herself a glass of wine. On hearing the cork getting popped, the others held out their empty glasses.

"How was your day?" Emma asked.

Kendal described their idyllic tour of the vast resort, punctuated by a long, boozy lunch on the deck of a mountaintop restaurant. At the mention on their pizza slices, Emma shuddered.

"How did you leave it with the weirdo?" Bella asked. "Are you having another lesson tomorrow?"

"No way," she said. "I have to work. My boss is like a rottweiler for a new client, and he's fuming that I'm on holiday."

Kendal dressed in a pressed blue shirt and chinos, with brogues that slid like skates when he stepped onto the snow. Emma – in her only outfit of jeans, hiking boots and the jumper from her dad – took her boyfriend's hand to steady him.

"Couldn't you find any shops today?" Kendal asked.

"No. Is it bad? We are only going to a bar, right?" Emma said, brushing the wool of her jumper flat.

Kendal mumbled something that Emma couldn't quite catch.

"At least you're warm," Bella said with a smile, her legs bare beneath the hemline of a long faux fur coat.

The group kicked through the slush of the pedestrianised village, stepping aside now and then for a brave cyclist or horse-drawn carriage. Kendal tried in vain to avoid his shoes sinking into the snow up to his bare ankles. In a side street near the town square, Charlie held the door open to Caspers.

The bar was packed, and loud enough that conversations required leaning in and shouting. The floor was wet with beer and the air hot and humid from the ski jackets slung on the backs of chairs. Servers waltzed through the crowd with trays of lager balanced impossibly above their heads. Charlie made the universal sign for 'I'm getting drinks', and the rest of them managed to find a few vacant stools around a repurposed barrel.

Bella took off her coat to reveal a figure-hugging dress. She looked around for a peg, and then folded it over her forearm instead. Kendal leaned onto their table, but immediately lifted his arm to find his elbow was soaked. Around them were groups of young snowboarders who had come straight off the mountain.

"Shall we go somewhere else?" Kendal asked. "It's a bit ... grubby."

Emma laughed. "It's fun," she said. "How did you hear about it?"

"Alice said it was where all the cool kids hang out. I didn't realise she meant actual kids."

Charlie weaved back from the bar, a clutch of drinks squeezed precariously in his fingers. "Did you tell Emma about the apartment?" He asked Kendal as he set the drinks down.

"Ah," said Kendal. "Of course! I forgot to say. This afternoon we popped into an estate agent and looked at a few sales sheets. Then we got talking and he showed us a model of some apartments they're hoping to build. It looks stunning. Pool in the basement, hot tubs outside. Ten-minute walk to town."

"Oh wow," said Emma. "What stage is it at?"

"They've identified the plot and hope to break ground this year. They're looking for investment."

"Kendal's going to buy it," Bella gushed.

"Maybe," he said. "Probably. It's such a faff doing the ski rental."

Bella clapped excitedly. Kendal stirred his drink, a smug grin stretching across his face. He looked to Emma for a reaction.

"Go you," she said. "That's very exciting. Would anyone like to dance?"

Kendal turned to look at the packed dance floor, steam rising into the ceiling lights like smoke. He shuddered and looked at Emma as if she were insane.

"Bella?" Emma asked, pulling her jumper over her head. She considered putting it on the table for a moment, then passed it to Kendal for safekeeping. The boys watched their partners slink off into the crowd, arms above their heads.

"You've done well, there, mate," Kendal said wistfully, sipping his drink.

Charlie looked at him with furrowed brow.

"And you. Who'd have thought the two of us would end up with such beauties."

Kendal sniggered.

"What's up, Kendal; are you two not getting on?"

Kendal shrugged. "I don't know. Yes. No. It's just hard, isn't it?"

Charlie thought for a moment, sucking in his lower lip.

"Which bit's hard, K? The luxury penthouse giving you vertigo? Sashimi falling from your chopsticks?"

Charlie punched his friend on the upper arm, but Kendal remained hunched over his glass, drawing lines in the condensation with his thumb.

"Emma's great fun," Charlie reminded him.

Kendal sighed and swilled the last drops of his drink, the ice cube wetting his upper lip.

"If I wanted fun, I would have got a dog," he said.

"Wow," said Charlie. "That bad?"

"It's alright for you. You've got Bella."

Charlie looked quizzically at Kendal. He continued.

"Clue is in the name. She's beautiful. You've done well, that's all."

"Have you *seen* Emma?" Charlie said. "She's gorgeous."

"And yet she manages to hide it under hiking boots and tatty jumpers," Kendal said, raising it up like a rag. "Anyway, mustn't complain. I'm buying property. That always cheers me up."

Charlie nodded, still a little shocked by the outburst.

"Retail therapy, I think they call it," he said.

At the end of the bar, Emma and Bella caught their breath over bottles of Corona with limes jammed in the neck. The place had a rawness about it; metal ducting exposed across the ceiling, stickers from ski and mountain bike brands all over the walls. It took Emma back to her first year of university, in a brief whirlwind of hedonism before she found herself consumed by textbooks.

"Why are we drinking beer?" asked Bella, chinking her bottle excitedly against Emma's.

"Just wanted a change." Emma shrugged. "Kendal insists that we drink wine that has been stored at exactly 12.7 degrees for forty-two years. The other day he spent a grand on a bottle of brandy that had been raised from a shipwreck."

"How did it taste?" Bella asked, wiping a bead of sweat from her forehead.

"Oh, it's not for drinking. It's to be left on the side, casually sitting among some other bottles, just proud enough that Kendal can tell every person the story. Amazon delivery at the door? Kendal's like 'Oh that old thing? It's from a shipwreck'."

Bella laughed.

"You're funny, Emma. I can see why Kendal's so fond of you."

"Well, you must tell him some time," Emma said. "I'm not very fun at the moment, and I can tell it's rubbing off on Kendal. I just get so into my work, and then I get stressed out and maybe a bit mean."

"You're definitely fun, Emma. Everyone gets a bit stressed out with work now and then. "I know I did."

"What's it like; not working?" Emma asked.

"It's like a massage I never want to end," Bella told her, staring into space.

"Do you ever get bored?" Emma asked.

"Sure I do. But then I go shopping. And I never, ever get bored of that."

They both laughed and Bella took another sip of her drink.

"You should try it. Take some time off and enjoy yourself."

Emma shook her head.

"I couldn't do it to my mum," she said. "She wanted me so badly to be a lawyer."

"As long as you're both happy," Bella said. "Hey, isn't that your ski instructor?" She nudged Emma and nodded towards the far side of the room. "You didn't tell me he was hot!"

Leon was laughing with a friend in a graffitied corner, beneath a television which blasted out snowboarding. Without his ski jacket, Emma could see that his upper body was muscular and defined in a V-necked white t-shirt. His tousled hair was drawn back on his head, matted, she presumed, by a day beneath his beanie. His fringe had escaped, though, and hung around his eyes in sharp, dark blades. She conceded that he might be considered hot, in a rugged sort of way, but wouldn't go as far as to say it out loud. His eyes caught her stare, and he hopped down excitedly from his stool.

"Oh balls," Emma muttered. "He's coming over."

"Hi Emma," Leon said, excitedly. "We ski tomorrow?"

He crouched down and made a ski motion, knees together and swinging his upper body left and right. He was back in kindergarten mode, which meant at least he wouldn't start asking about her sex life.

"No, Leon. I'm going to have the day off. My legs will be aching," she said. "Maybe another time."

His face fell in disappointment. Leon signalled to the bartender, and looked at Bella and Emma, who shook their heads.

"You don't like skiing?" he said.

"It wasn't a great day, if I'm honest," she said.

"Because you suck at skiing," he said. "But you will get better. It was your first day."

Bella sniggered, but Emma's jaw dropped.

"Leon, you're crass, and rude. Instead of teaching me to ski, you just say 'pizza, pizza, pizza', and then rugby tackle me into a pile of snow," she said.

He chuckled at the memory.

"That's my job. Should I have let you ski into the people waiting at the lift?" he asked.

"No, you should have taught me to stop before setting me off down a hill."

"Gemma!" a voice interrupted them.

Emma spun around just in time to see Alice stagger toward her with a bottle of prosecco hanging from her hand. Alice swung her free arm around Emma's shoulder in an embrace that nearly toppled them both.

"Alice. Happy birthday," she said. "And it's Emma."

The chalet host's eyes were bleary and distant, and her lipstick smeared on her lower lip. She looked at Leon and gave him a playful pout.

"Happy birthday, Alice," he nodded.

"Do you two know each other?" Emma asked.

"Of course. Everyone knows Alice," Leon grinned.

"Easy now," Alice said, leaning against the bar. "Emma, your other half is up there. He don't mess around."

She raised her bottle and glass, and attempted to refill it, with moderate success. Emma and Bella spotted Kendal across the bar and set off toward him.

"Goodbye, Leon," Emma said over her shoulder. "I won't be needing any more ski lessons."

"You really will," he said.

"Thanks a lot," she said.

Chapter Nine

♥

E mma was woken by a laser of sunlight which cut through the gap in the curtains and sliced across their vast bed. On a workday, it would have caused her to hide under the pillow, but drifting into holiday mode, she just rolled out of its path. She raised her head above Kendal's chest, to check the time on the bedside clock. 7:30am. He stirred, and she rested her cheek on his chest, gentry running her hand across the contours of his torso.

He mechanically kissed the top of her head, then peeled back the covers and stretched before leaving the bed. The sound of his electric toothbrush meant he was not planning to return, and she opened the bathroom door. Emma leaned against the doorway, wrapped in a duvet and gently biting at the inside of cheek.

"Kendal, are we okay?" she asked.

He looked at her appraisingly, and then spat out a mouthful of toothpaste.

"What do you mean?"

He sat on the edge of the bed, pulling ski socks over his feet. Emma sat beside him, dropping her head low to get into his line of sight..

"I mean, do you still fancy me?" she said, realising a little too late that she was cocooned in a duvet and looked like a tortoise.

"Emma, why would I bring you to a place like this if I didn't?"

She smiled and gave his thigh a gentle squeeze. The muscles tensed as he arose, slipping out onto the landing wearing only boxers and socks.

"Kendal, have you forgotten something?" she said.

He looked down.

"Salopettes are in the drying room," he said. "I'll bring yours up too."

"That's okay, I'm not going up today," Emma sighed as she crawled back into the bed.

The chalet bustled with activity and she closed her eyes and picked out the sounds of its cast. Bella's light footsteps on the stairs. The guys' brotherly back slaps. Alice shouting 'wahey' as Kendal passed through the kitchen, half-dressed.

Emma picked up her phone. The red notification symbol on her unread messages gave her a pang of anxiety, but leaving them unopened was unthinkable. Email volleys about the new Swiss client had piled up overnight, and with every reply she felt herself being edged into irrelevance. To try to claw her way back into the conversation would require hours of reading and analysis, which felt impossible without her laptop.

A few minutes later, she smelled bacon and pulled on one of Kendal's shirts as she headed downstairs. Alice was in the kitchen, deftly overseeing a hob packed with frying pans. Bella, Kendal, and Charlie – now fully dressed - were at the table. Alice took a plate from the cupboard and looked to Emma, spatula aloft.

"Mushrooms? Tomatoes?" Alice said.

"Yes please," Emma replied. "It all looks delicious."

Kendal coughed loudly to get his girlfriend's attention and pointed over at the lounge. Poking up above the back of a tan leather couch was a mop of chestnut hair. Emma narrowed her eyes and looked at her friends.

"It's the weirdo," Bella mouthed. "Kendal let him in."

"Leon?" Emma whispered in alarm.

The trio nodded. Amid the clatter of porcelain and frying pans, she could hear the faint sound of his snores.

Emma put her plate down on the worktop and slipped back upstairs with quiet, feline steps. She returned a few minutes later in a pair of jeans and with her hair tied back in a ponytail. She took her breakfast to the dining table, from which she could see Leon's face. Eyes shut, mouth agape.

"Alice, what's he doing here?" Emma said quietly.

"Oh, Leon? I saw him on the walk over. He said he might as well meet you here and you could go to the lifts together."

He woke suddenly, knocking an empty coffee cup from the table as he started. It banged on the rug and rolled in an arc.

"Sorry," he said, returning it to the table upside down. He looked over at the dining area, where all four of the chalet's guests were tucking into breakfast.

Leon wore the same baggy ski trousers as the day before, his socks drooping past the ends of his feet. His jacket gaped open, its pockets stuffed with mittens, goggles, and his hat. He ran his hand through his hair, which was just long enough to stay put behind his ears. His stubble cast a shadow across his darkly tanned face.

"Hi Emma," he said. "And Emma's friends."

"Charlie, Bella, Kendal.' Emma said with a sigh as she made introductions. "This is Leon, and he was just leaving."

"We have a lesson booked for this morning." Leon raised his cup hopefully as Alice passed by with orange juice and coffee.

"Leon, do you not remember last night?" Emma said.

He looked across at Alice.

"Bits and pieces," he said.

Alice clattered some pans noisily as she tidied up. She refilled the orange juice and coffee of the guests. Leon flipped the cup over and raised it, hopefully, but Alice ignored him.

"Leon, we met at the bar. I said I wasn't going to be skiing today. I have to work," Emma said.

"Why? You're on a ski holiday, no?"

Kendal sniggered. "I mean, he's right, Em'. You might as well go now. Work can wait."

Emma sighed, continuing her breakfast to refuel before responding. Leon watched her back, until she finally turned and spoke to him like a primary school teacher, eyebrows raised.

"Will you be reasonable? Yesterday you pushed me over. You ate my lunch. You confiscated my phone."

Kendal and Charlie laughed, and then Leon joined in. Even Alice, listening in from the kitchen, couldn't hide her amusement. Emma looked around, outnumbered.

"Fine. Fine. I'll get ready," she said.

After a long and mostly silent walk to the lifts, Emma bought a lift pass and stopped at a kiosk for two cups of coffee. She passed one to Leon, who took it gratefully. The two of them clipped in and shuffled toward the chairlift, which Emma boarded without much fuss.

The sky was overcast, and snow sat heavily on grey-blue spruce boughs beneath their feet. Emma pulled her hat over her ears, and placed her goggles over that.

"Paprika," he muttered.

She raised her eyebrows.

"We call that colour paprika," he reiterated, motioning toward her hat.

"Oh, good comeback Leon. From *yesterday*. So, why were you at our chalet; is this your way of avoiding cancellations?"

He shrugged.

"I didn't remember you cancelling. I went home from the bar with Alice. She woke me up early because she had to cook breakfast, and so I thought I would come straight to you. No point going home."

"So, you haven't been home for 24 hours?" she asked.

Emma attempted to shuffle over on the bench seat but was blocked by the safety bar. The chairlift whirred gently as it ascended, clunking as they passed each tower.

"So, Alice had a good birthday then," Emma said.

Leon cocked his head to the side, then smirked when her insinuation landed.

"Oh, yes. Her birthday," he said.

"Is that funny?" Emma asked.

"She has a birthday every Wednesday. She must be a hundred years old."

"Oh, I see," said Emma, realising her naivety.

She pinched the fingertip of her mitten with her teeth and pulled it off, reaching into her pocket for her phone. She tapped a message to Kendal.

"I wouldn't," Leon said.

"Message my boyfriend?"

Leon shrugged. "If you drop it from the lift, you'll never see it again."

"I'm sure I can manage. I need to tell Kendal we've been duped."

A minute later, it pinged. She chuckled and returned it to her pocket, tapping her thigh to demonstrate it was safely stowed.

"What did he say?" Leon asked.

"If you must know, he said that she is a very bad girl."

Leon whistled quietly. "Yes. She really is."

Emma shook her head as if to kick the mental image from her mind.

· ♥ · ♥ · ♥ · ♥ · ♥ ·

"The snow is soft today," Leon said. "So, you have nothing to worry about if you fall into it. We need to work on speed."

Emma clipped her skis in and looked down the hill anxiously.

"It's not the snow I'm worried about. It's everything else. Trees, people, lifts."

She waved her pole about to point out all the potential hazards that seemed to litter the slope.

"Okay but trust me. If you go a bit faster, then your skis will do the work. It's like riding a bike. If you go too slowly, you fall."

Emma looked unconvinced but put her skis into a wide V-shape and jabbed her poles into the snow to get moving. She began to inch down the hill at a glacial pace. Leon shook his head in frustration.

"No, no, no. This is no good," he said. "Bring the heels together. Imagine I have stolen your phone."

She moved them a touch, but her snow plough remained so wide that she barely moved. Leon slid in from behind, his skis nesting in between hers. He docked gently against her and placed his hands on her hips. With his extra weight, they began to pick up speed, as one.

"What are you doing?" she panicked, looking down at the snow rushing beneath her.

"Look up!" he said. "Look all the way down the slope at where we are going and relax."

"Relax?" she shouted.

They cruised down the shallow green run, and Emma began to get comfortable with the speed.

Leon swung his ski pole toward a chairlift to their right, further downslope.

"Look at that lift and put pressure on your left ski," he instructed.

"You're pointing to the right. You mean my right ski," she said. Emma leaned into her right ski and they began to snake to the left. With Leon leaning one way and Emma the other, their skis became entangled. Leon's boots jammed into Emma's, and they tumbled together onto the slope, spinning like turtles on their backs.

Emma laughed, surprising herself. She sat up and pulled the goggles away from her face to pick the snow out.

"I know my left and right," Leon said. "If I say left, I mean left."

"Okay, grumpy guts," she said, stumbling down the slope to retrieve a ski that had gone on its own adventure.

She attempted to click it back in, but the underside of her boot was thick with ice. Leon told her to sit down and began to chip it off using the top of his ski pole.

"Did you call *me* grumpy? Emma, you have to trust me," he said.

"Says the man who, uninvitedly..." she searched for a delicate way to put it, and eventually went with the inevitable. "Takes me from behind."

He furrowed his brows.

"Doesn't matter," she said, catching his smile. "I'm not saying it again." She clambered to her feet and got into a wide V-shape, once again inching downslope at a snail's pace. Leon muttered something to himself, which she couldn't hear above the sound of her skis on the snow. She looked back.

"Go on then," she said.

He smiled and skated down to catch her up. Emma squealed with anxiety as he approached, faster than before, and slid in behind her, his pelvis docking gently into her bum. She giggled as the two of them careened down the hill, leaning in unison this time to steer toward the chairlift. Second time round, they made it to the base of the slope in one piece.

"Okay. Off now," she said, wiggling away from him.

Emma and Leon warmed themselves in a quiet slope side restaurant. Tucked at the base of a quiet wooded run, the hut was almost empty. They waited quietly for Emma's meal and Leon's tap water, listening to the crackle of a log burner and occasional creak of ski boots. A waitress set an onion tart onto the table in front of Leon and Emma pulled the plate toward her protectively.

"So, your boyfriend is rich as a sheikh, and yet you wear a homemade jumper," Leon said. "What's up with that?"

Taking advantage of Emma's pause to process the question, Leon reached across the table and extracted a French fry from her stack. She slapped his hand like a fly, crushing his plunder. He straightened the chip out and ate it.

"My dad made me this jumper, so it's very special to me," she said.

He nodded. "You cannot beat mother nature. She had millions of years to make a material that is not too hot, not too cold. Waterproof enough, but not too heavy."

Emma nodded, rotating her plate so that the fries faced Leon. He widened his eyes with delight, and she nodded. He laid out a napkin and shovelled them in like a bank robber.

"If we're being nosy, how come you can afford to drink at the bar, but not buy lunch?" she asked.

"Because I can only afford the essentials. I'm kidding. I don't really drink at the bar, I just go there after work to see friends. I'm saving up at the moment."

Emma hoisted her sleeves to her elbows and ate her tart in small forkfuls to make it last longer.

"So if you weren't drinking, you must remember talking to me at Caspers last night? I said I wasn't going to ski today."

He nodded.

"But I knew deep down that Fun Emma *did* want to ski today, so I had to come and get you."

"Like a knight in yesterday's armour." she said. "Anyway, what makes you think Kendal's rich as a king? What did he tell you?"

"I never spoke to him. Alice told me he bought her a bottle of champagne. That's quite the move in Caspers."

"Did he now?" Emma asked.

The fries gone, Leon sat back and dried out the lenses of his goggles with his cuff.

"So, are you and Alice...close?" Emma pried. She focused on her delicate tart, eager not to appear preoccupied by such gossip.

"Like family, you mean?" Leon asked.

"No. I mean, you spent the night with her. I suppose I'm asking if you two are an item. A couple."

He shook his head vigorously.

"No. Last night I left the bar when it closed and I saw her sitting on a bench, singing to herself. I said to her you will die out here at night, and she laughed. I practically carried her to her apartment, and I slept on the couch."

"Really?" asked Emma, throwing him a suspicious grin.

"Why would I lie?" Leon shrugged. "I stayed over because I thought Alice might choke on her own vomit. It most definitely was not sexy time."

At the thought of Alice being sick, Emma rested her cutlery against the lip of the plate. Her phone buzzed and she peered at the screen.

"What time will we be done?" she asked Leon.

"Skiing?" he said.

She nodded.

"Last lift is four-o-clock," he said.

She tapped a response and they both heard the swoosh as the message sent. Emma resumed her lunch.

"Kendal?" he asked.

"Yes, he's too hungover to ski. They've gone back to the chalet."

She smiled and slipped the phone back into her top pocket.

"He must miss me," she said.

As they ascended a chairlift, the falling snow gathered along their skis in neat white Toblerones. Emma pulled up her hood to stop the flakes from going down her neck. She watched two skiers snake down the mountain in a synchronised figure-of-eight, carving neat trenches in the fresh powder.

"Charlie! Bella!" shouted Emma.

One of the skiers skidded to a stop with a spray of snow. He looked up and waved. Bella joined him.

"See you at the chalet later," they shouted.

Emma watched them continue their run; Charlie racing ahead with broad sketchy arcs, and Bella springing from side to side with beautiful, neat technique.

"Ugh. I need to get good," Emma announced urgently. "Teach me, Leon."

He laughed.

"I try, Emma. But you are very cautious."

"I won't be any more," she announced. "I've had lunch. I'm a different person after I've eaten. Like a T-Rex. I want to get good so I can ski with the others."

"Is my company so bad?" Leon asked. Emma didn't respond, and he continued, "Okay, this afternoon we will work on smooth, carving turns. Normally you should master snow plough, but this soft snow is perfect for learning. And you need to get good so you can ski with your sugar daddy."

He raised his eyebrows, waiting for a response.

"How dare you," she said. "I don't let him pay for anything."

"I thought you said he paid for this holiday."

"It was a birthday present," she muttered.

Leon smiled.

Beneath them, snow-capped fir trees pointed skyward like rockets on a launchpad. Emma tugged a mitten from her hand and carefully withdrew her phone from her pocket.

"Don't worry," she said to Leon.

She went to reinsert it into her pocket, but it slipped from her cold wet fingertips. The phone bounced on the black foam seat and before she could grab it, it slid through a gap between the seat. In silence, it shot down into a mass of dense trees and disappeared.

Leon shook his head.

"Damn," Emma said, eyes wide, gripping the metal bar as she stared down. "We can find it, right?" she said, an edge of desperation in her voice as she turned to Leon.. "27. It's just downslope of tower 27. We can ski down there and search, can't we?"

"We cannot ski down there," Leon said. "It's too dangerous."

"But I need it."

"Why did you get it out?" Leon said. "I told you this would happen."

"God you sound like Kendal," Emma snapped. "You were right. Okay? I'm an idiot. And now I have no laptop and no phone, and probably no job to go back to."

The wind whistled across their chairlift. Emma leaned onto the metal bar and buried her face in the crook of her elbow.

Chapter Ten

♥

T hey sat on the snow until the cold made Emma's bum go numb. Leon had been uncharacteristically quiet, making no comment as a tear escaped her eye.

"It's not just a phone," she said, finally. "I mean it is. But there are messages on there - not only from work..." her voice trailed off as she thought about the long thread of messages and photos she had sent to her mother's number over the years.

"I'm sorry." Leon placed a gentle hand on her shoulder, and she looked down at it in shock.

"But you hated me using it." She met his eyes and his face was serious, for once, with something she could only describe as concern in his expression.

"Yes." He shrugged. "But it was important to you."

She stared at him a moment longer, the warmth from his hand seeping through her jacket, before suddenly standing up and brushing herself off.

"Okay. Let's ski," she said, taking a deep breath. "There's no point feeling sorry for myself anymore. Fun Emma is back."

At the top of a shallow green run, Emma stamped into her skis. The snow fell so heavily that her cheeks were wet.

"When you crash in this snow, it won't even hurt," Leon said.

"Why would I crash?" Emma asked.

"Because we are skiing. It happens."

"I'm kidding," she said. "I fall every five metres." She looked over at him until his face cracked into a smile.

Leon put his index fingers side by side, pointing up like rockets.

"We are going to keep our skis parallel and lean on the outside to make one big carve from right to left. You will go a little faster than before, but commit to the turn and it will work. If you end up going too fast..."

"....You'll tackle me to the floor like a store detective?" she said.

"Yes. Go!"

Emma cautiously began her descent, keeping her skis initially parallel before instinctively jamming them into a V-shape to scrub off speed. It took several attempts, but eventually she managed to hold her nerve and keep the skis evenly spaced. As Leon had predicted, she began to carve in a huge arc, back to a stop at the left side of the piste. With burning thighs, she collapsed to the ground with a grin across her face.

"That was great, Emma," Leon said. "Let's go. One more. Opposite way."

Emma set off once again but failed to initiate the turn. Time and again she tried, but only managed to pick up speed and wobble back to the left side of the slope.

"You're not putting pressure on your left ski," Leon said, stamping his boot to illustrate the cure.

"I am. It just doesn't work," she said, laying at the edge of the piste. She listened to her angry heartbeat and watched the fresh flakes float onto her goggles. Leon crouched at her feet and unclipped the buckles on her right boot.

"What are you doing? Tightening my boots won't help," she said.

He yanked the plastic tongue away from her shin, and using her ski for leverage, pulled the entire boot from her foot. Her heel dropped onto the cold white ground, and snowflakes stuck on the pink fibres of her sock. Leon jammed the ski into the snow beyond Emma's reach.

"Give me my boot back!" she said. "My foot is freezing."

He pulled her up, and she managed to limp onto her one ski, with two poles providing support. Her right foot hung in the air, knee bent.

"Give me my boot back!" she shouted. "This isn't funny."

"Come and get it," he said, skiing across to the right-hand side of the slope.

"Leon!" she shouted. Other skiers whizzed down between them, laughing at the bickering couple.

Emma began to slide on her remaining ski, and for the first time in her brief skiing life, she looked up from the ground beneath her to stare – with venomous eyes – at Leon. As he predicted, the ski bit into the snow and carved smoothly across to the right-hand side. Unable to stop, she careened straight into Leon and toppled him to the ground. He laughed as she snatched her ski and boot and rolled over, eagerly pulling it back over her freezing foot.

"You can't just tear women's clothes off!" she said. "It's 2024."

"It worked, though, didn't it?" he grinned.

"Oh, shut up, Mr Miyagi," she said.

Emma clipped her boot shut and skied off, pleased with her newfound competence but unwilling to give Leon one ounce of credit.

"Are you still mad at me about the boot?" Leon asked.

Emma, sitting at the top of a gentle green ski slope, shook her head.

"Well, yes. But it's something else."

He waited, and she sighed quietly, annoyed to be pushed into sharing her thoughts with this neanderthal.

"Kendal said *we* are heading down. But then I saw Charlie and Bella, and I wanted to double check I had read it right. That's when I dropped my phone."

"He went down on his own. So what?" Leon asked.

"Nothing. Exactly. Let's ski."

Emma stood up, which at 2pm took a Herculean effort. Her thighs felt like she had climbed to the top of the Statue of Liberty.

"Oh," said Leon, as if he now understood.

Emma wiped a dusting of snow from the sepia goggle lenses and looked at him through the water streaks that remained. She raised a hand as if to say 'what?'

"Nothing," Leon said. "Let's ski."

He positioned Emma so that she could complete another long, slow turn, this time to the right. She put pressure on her outside ski, as before, and the deep snow and shallow slope meant she was able to complete a satisfying curve without picking up too much speed.

"Emma, that was great!" Leon said, clapping with genuine excitement. He skied down to catch up.

"What were you thinking?" she asked. "When you said 'oh'."

"That maybe you don't trust him," he said.

"I do," Emma said defensively. "He's probably tired. Wants a nap."

"Has he cheated on you before?" Leon asked.

"Well that's none of your business."

He raised both hands in a peace offering. "I know. I'm sorry."

The duo set off once more, with Leon skiing backwards and encouraging Emma to lean into her turn and not panic.

The snowfall became heavier, floating down in great beautiful flakes. At half past two, Emma spotted the gondola that returned to the village.

"Leon, I'm going to head down at the end of this run," she said. "The snow is too heavy for me."

"Okay," he said. "Am I still fired? Or just you."

She reverted to a safe snowplough to tackle the last hundred metres to the lift. "What difference does it make?" she shouted as she slid away from him. "You'll just turn up anyway."

He laughed, and watched her inch toward the gondola. When she reached it without incident, he cheered. She ignored him, but remained conscious of his gaze as she slung her skis onto her shoulder and clunked up the steps into the bubble lift.

Having learned her lesson the day before, Emma left her ski equipment at the rental shop and walked home in blissfully comfortable hiking boots. Back at the chalet, she padded upstairs in her socks, leaving a trail of single wet footprints from where Leon had removed her ski boot halfway up the mountain. The lounge was empty, and she opened the cupboard door quietly so as not to wake her boyfriend of two years. An ornate box from a cake shop sat on the worktop, and she decided against piercing the seal and tucking in.

Faintly, she heard a noise from upstairs. Emma cocked her head to one side and listened, this time picking out a knocking, and perhaps a woman's voice. She looked around for signs that Bella and Charlie had returned but couldn't see their jackets on the hook. She crept upstairs and felt a wave of nausea pass over her as she heard the distinct sound of a woman's moans and exhalations coming from her bedroom.

Emma closed her eyes and pursed her lips. Tears formed in the corners as she gripped the door handle. She pressed it down and swung it open, to see Kendal's bum, thrusting forward and back. Blond hair splayed across her pillow, like rays of the sun.

Kendal spun around, and beneath him, Alice yanked the duvet across her.

"Emma!" he shrieked.

She scowled at him with murderous eyes and slammed the door shut.With her back against the landing wall, her legs gave way and she slid to the floor. Her heaving breaths masked the noise of the two miscreants racing to get dressed. The door opened and Alice scurried out like a cockroach, tears rolling down her cheeks. Emma heard the front door slam as she left.

"Emma, please," Kendal appeared in the doorway in his bathrobe. Emma stormed past him into the bedroom, arm over her lower face to block the sickly smell of sweat.

She wrenched the wardrobe door open and looked around, before remembering she didn't have a suitcase to pack. She marched around to her side of the bed, stuffing her passport into the pocket of her ski trousers.

"Emma, I'm so sorry," Kendal said. "I don't know what I was thinking."

"Fuck you, Kendal! Don't tell me..." Emma snapped. "*It's not what it seems.*"

She wiped the tears on the sleeve of her jumper and pulled what few possessions she had from the top drawer; a few pairs of ski socks, underwear and nightwear that Bella had given her. She clutched them to her chest and left the room.

"Where are you going?" Kendal said, following her onto the landing. "We can talk about this."

Emma raced down the stairs, nearly slipping as her socks slid against the varnished pine treads.

"I'm leaving you," she said. "Like I should have done the first time."

Emma rooted through the kitchen for a bag, and eventually found a bin liner under the sink. She stuffed her clothes into it and slung the box of cakes in too. She kicked on her hiking shoes, stamping the heel down at the back, and grabbed her jacket from the peg, still wet from skiing.

Kendal dashed down the stairs, tapping away at his phone.

"I don't understand," he said. "Why is it saying you're still up the mountain?"

Emma stood in the doorway, shaking her head in disbelief.

"I'm so sorry, Kendal, that I lost my phone. That must have really ruined your afternoon. I'll try to be more considerate next time!"

She slammed the door behind her, but it made a less than satisfying thwump where the modern rubber seals received the triple glazed door. As if to compensate, Emma screamed toward the sky. She slung the bin liner over her shoulder and marched away from the chalet, demolishing every footprint left by Alice minutes before.

Chapter Eleven

♥

"There must be something," Emma said. "I've tried six hotels. They all said try you."

The receptionist sucked through his teeth and turned up his palms, helplessly.

"It is *the* busiest week of the season," he explained. "School holidays in Switzerland. We have been booked up for months. There is nothing. Have you tried searching online?"

"I don't have a phone. Can you search for me?" she said.

Other guests crossed the marble-floored lobby, dressed smartly for dinner. He looked at the bin liner on the floor beside Emma, and then seemed to stare right through her. Emma looked confused, then turned to see a bellman who had been called to assist.

"Let me help you out with your belongings, ma'am," he said, lifting up her sack and shepherding her toward the revolving door.

Emma stared up and down the street outside the hotel. The lamps were now on and the last train to the valley had long since departed. She felt unable to take another step and sat on a bench outside the ski rental shop. Inside her jacket pocket, Emma felt the soft material of her coral-coloured beanie and pulled it hard over her ears. All around her the ski racks were empty, and the rental store was dark inside. She tapped on the glass in case someone was in the back, but there was nothing.

Through teary eyes, she looked at her reflection in the glass. She had a faint white outline of goggles around her eyes from the day before, when the sun had shone. As she turned to look up and down the street for the tenth time, she noticed the paper taped to the inside of the window, with the words SKI INSTRUCTOR. She closed her eyes and let her head fall slowly toward the glass. For a moment she rested there, her breath condensing on the freezing pane.

Emma left her bag by the bench and returned to the posh hotel she had most recently tried.

"Madame, I'm afraid I cannot let you enter," said the concierge.

"Just give me a pen and a piece of paper, " she said. "Then I'll be out of your hair."

He huffed but withdrew a Four Seasons pen from his desk and tore a Post-It note from a pad. She returned a few minutes later.

"I came to return your pen," she said.

"Oh. That wasn't necessary, but thank you," he replied.

"May I use your phone?" she said.

"I'm afraid telephones are for the guests," he said.

"Oh, come on!" Emma said, raising her voice. The receptionist glanced around nervously. Emma leaned in and spoke more quietly.

"It's snowing outside and I cannot go back to my chalet. I'm asking you, as a considerate human being, to let me make a phone call. I need a place to stay. I'm desperate."

She slid the note across the counter, and he rotated it. He tapped the numbers into his phone, and when it started to ring, passed it to Emma.

When it was finally answered, Emma had to hold it away from her ear because the pulsating beat was deafening.

"Where are you?" Emma said.

"Hello?" Leon shouted.

"Where. Are. You?" Emma repeated.

The receptionist reached across for his phone, desperate to shut the noisy conversation down. Emma pulled away, stretching the coiled cable until the Four Seasons employee had to hold down his base unit to stop it being dragged off the desk.

"You want a ski lesson?" Leon said. "I cannot hear you."

"Where are you, Leon? It's Emma."

There was a pause, and Emma could only hear the pounding Euro dance music.

"Emma?" Leon shouted. "Okay. Meet me at the lift. 9am."

"No, Leon. Now!"

He laughed. The music boomed, glasses chinked.

"It is too late to ski now. It is party time. See you in the morning."

"Please Leon, don't hang up!" Emma said.

The line went dead.

"Leon?" Emma said hopelessly. With a quivering hand, she placed the receiver into the concierge's outstretched hand. She scooped up her bin liner and was ushered out of the hotel once more.

With Emma's last lifeline depleted, she looked up the hill toward Kendal's ski chalet. She breathed firmly through her nose and exhaled a long, sad breath that hung in the cold night air like smoke. She made an almost inaudible scream, just for herself to hear, and made her first, sad steps toward the chalet.

"Hey Santa," came a voice from behind her. She turned around slowly; too shattered both physically and emotionally to respond any faster. It was Leon, panting, in his baggy ski pants and jacket zipped up to his chin.

"What is going on?" he asked.

Emma dropped her sack onto the ground and began to sob. Leon rushed toward her, grabbing her elbows, and stooped to look into her eyes.

"What happened?" he asked.

"Kendal cheated on me. I left. But there are no hotels anywhere, trains are finished. And I don't have a phone. And everything's just gone to shit," she said.

"Oh, Emma," he said softly.

She wiped her eyes with shaking hands and took a shuddering breath. "I just called to see if you could let me use your phone," she told him as his hands moved comfortingly up and down her arms, as though he was trying to keep her warm. "I need to look up a hotel. There has to be a room available somewhere."

He shook his head.

"It is school holidays, everywhere is booked up." He let go of her and gathered up her bin liner, spinning the bag below into a sphere before slinging it over his shoulder. "So, you want a ski lesson?" he said.

She looked at him incredulously. He gathered up the lip of her bin liner and held it in his fist, spinning the bag below into a sphere.

"I'm joking," he said. "Let's go!"

Leon set off down the street, head down to shield his face from the falling snow. Emma followed, pulling her goggles over her eyes to give her face a little protection from the biting night air.

"Where are we going?" she said.

"Emma, there are three beds for you in this town. Your boyfriend's, if you want a threesome. The hospital, which is where you'll end up if you stay outside. Or my cabin. You choose."

She thought for a moment, waiting for a fourth option to magically appear, but she knew he was right. She let out a sigh and then jogged after him to catch up.

They walked down the main street, past crowded bars and a pharmacy sign that blazed neon green against the night sky. The pools of light from street lamps ended abruptly and they trudged on into the darkness through thick snow, lit only by the glow from ski chalets set back from the road. Leon paused by a gap between buildings and pulled a torch from his pocket. He pointed it at a thick, black forest that surrounded the road.

"We're going in there?" Emma gulped.

"Mind where you step," he said, wading into knee deep powder.

Emma stepped carefully into the bomb holes that Leon's huge boots left in the snow. It took great effort for her to lift her tired legs and make lunar steps. After several minutes, she looked up and saw only splashes of light on tall trunks lit by Leon's head torch. Behind her there was no trace of humanity, only darkness.

"Leon, where are we going? I don't want to sound ungrateful, but I feel like I'm being abducted," she said.

"Keep up!" he shouted back at her. "This weather is no joke."

"Nor is abduction," she muttered, shuddering at the darkness that seemed to be enveloping her. She sprang forward to catch up with Leon and his tiny beam of light.

Finally, they came upon a forest clearing in which she could see the snow falling once more. In it was a single-storey log cabin with a steeply pitched roof and porthole windows. Leon climbed the few steps onto a veranda that wrapped around the building and dumped the bin liner by the front door. He pulled his boots off and stepped inside, holding the door open for Emma, who apprehensively followed him into the dark building.

Chapter Twelve

♥

L eon fumbled around the base of a lamp to twist the switch. A warm glow lit up the entrance, but it remained too dark inside to see much beyond the doormat and wooden floorboards. Leon swung his snowy boots onto a rack just by the front door and Emma did the same. He took her coat and hung it on a peg, but they both kept their beanies pulled firmly over their ears.

Protected from the icy wind, it was mildly warmer inside than out, but their breath still misted the air. Leon criss-crossed the room, turning on a few more lamps perched on side tables and stands. There was no ceiling light. He picked up a wide wicker basket and tutted.

"We are almost out of firewood," he said. "I'll go and get some."

He disappeared outside. Emma crouched by a black metal stove and found a wooden box with a lighter and kindling. She laid a bed of straw, then constructed a wigwam of twigs and logs. She carefully fed the lighter into the space she had left, and the fire crackled satisfyingly into life. Something brushed against her arm, and she shrieked.

A cat, grey and svelte, meowed, and she exhaled slowly to regain her composure.

Leon returned with a basket brimming with wood and stopped short when he saw the fire she had lit. "Thank you," he said, visibly impressed.

Emma surveyed the cabin properly for the first time. At one end of the long room was a rustic kitchen with deep blue cupboards and a sturdy wooden island. The beech worktop was cluttered but clean. A bunch of carrots, still with their whip of leaves. A loaf of homemade bread, wrapped loosely in a tea towel. In the middle of the room was a dining table with four chairs, arched backs over a fan of spindles. At the other end was a lounge, with a second log burner which Leon busied himself lighting.

"Make yourself at home," he said. "I'm sorry it's so cold. I cannot heat it while I am out all day." He closed the glass door of the stove but left it ajar so the nascent flames could breathe.

"It's fine. I like it." Emma said, surprising herself by the confession.

She sat cross-legged on a sheepskin rug in front of the wood burner, the cat gently headbutting her knees to get attention. Leon sat on a tatty sofa that seemed to swallow him up. He moved aside a hardback book about Alpine flowers and rested his feet in the space he had made.

"If I'd have known I was going to have company, I...Well to be honest I probably would have done nothing different."

Emma smiled. "I should hope not. Nobody wants one of those awful modern men who tidy up and buy their own lunch."

He chuckled and ran a hand through his hair, sweeping it back behind his ears.

Emma faced her palms to the stove.

"Leon, thanks so much for coming out of that bar tonight. I'd rather die of frostbite than have to walk back into that chalet."

The cat's tail tickled against her chin, making her stumble backwards.

"That's Jas," he said. "Jasmine Cat."

Jas nestled against Emma, who nuzzled the underside of the cat's jaw.

"She likes me," Emma said.

"I doubt that," Leon teased. "She is just cold."

"We'll see."

Emma and Leon sat quietly, watching the flames dance madly behind the stove's glass door. Now and then, Emma wore a thick glove and fed logs onto the stoves, and the wooden beams clicked and creaked as the cabin warmed.

Eventually Emma took off her hat and stuffed it in the pocket of jacket, which she hung alongside Leon's by the front door. She took her spot by the fire and toyed, sadly, with the tips of her long dark hair. Her eyes were glazed but she refused to cry.

"What happened?" Leon asked. She realised he was watching her from the lounge, and as she saw his chin resting on the ridge of the couch, it took her back to the start of her day.

"You know something weird?" she said. "I started today to unexpectedly find you asleep on my sofa. Honestly I thought 'What is he doing here?' Twelve hours later, you must be thinking the same thing about me."

He laughed loudly. Emma sighed, reliving the pivotal moment of her day.

"Alice," she said, morosely.

Leon nodded, and Emma noted his total lack of surprise.

"I'm sorry. How long had you been with him?" he asked.

"Two years."

Leon tutted, and offered a conciliatory smile. When he stood and stretched, his fingertips touched a thick oak beam that spanned the building, and his jumper lifted to reveal a slither of his tanned abs.

"Did you eat?" he asked, looking at his watch. "It's nine."

She shook her head.

"Now I feel really bad for eating your fries," he said.

She tried to smile, but her lips only thinned and drew inward. Leon walked across to the kitchen, taking the long way around the dining table to give her space. Emma watched him open the fridge, barren apart from a shelf of condiments and a door full of beer and milk. He took out a leftover sandwich wrapped in white paper and gave it a squeeze. It landed with a thud at the bottom of his bin. In a cupboard he rotated a couple of tins, sweetcorn, tuna, and other things that required some cooking, and closed the doors shut again.

"I'm embarrassed, Emma. I meant to do my shop today, but forgot. We could walk back into town and get something?" he said.

"No, honestly I'm fine," Emma said. "Can I just use the internet, and then I can check for hotel rooms."

He looked at her blankly.

"You have the internet, right?" she said.

"Emma, I don't even have a television. I have some beer, though?"

"Oh, I see. Can I look something up on your phone?" she asked.

He withdrew an ancient flip phone from his pocket and set it on the dining table. Emma smiled politely.

"You have to unfold it," he said.

"It doesn't have a browser, though, does it?" she asked.

"Browser? It has a really cool game where you grow a snake?" he said hopefully.

Emma looked at her bin liner of clothes that sat on a puddle of snowmelt by the door mat.

"I'll take that beer after all," she said.

Leon passed her a bottle and took one for himself. He pulled open the drawer to the freezer and withdrew a box of fish fingers.

"Look what I've found!" he said, twisting the knob on the oven to maximum with boyish excitement. She chuckled.

"Leon, are you sure you don't mind if I stay on the sofa?" she asked. "Tomorrow I will find a hotel or get an early flight home."

"Of course," he said. "I mean, it's that or certain death, so it would be a bit late now to say no. Relax, Emma. You had a bad day. You can have a shower if you want? I will turn on the hot water. The towels are in the cupboard under the sink."

Emma gratefully accepted the offer, and shivered as she removed her clothes in the bathroom. The shower, though, was blissfully warm, filling the room with steam. On the stone tray were several miniature bottles of shampoo and conditioner from high-end hotels. There was also a loafer brush and a natural sponge hanging from a hook. Emma disappointed herself by crying in there and wiped the tears away with a thick white towel embroidered with the Four Seasons logo. She had managed to keep her hair mostly out of the water, and dried her tips with a hairdryer she found under the sink.

With her bath sheet wrapped around her, she poked her head into the main room and asked Leon to pass her the bin liner. He did so, but it was so wide that she had to open the door fully to let it in. He grinned.

"Leon," she said, in a tone that someone might chastise a dog with its paws on the dining table.

"Oh. It's not that," he said, taking care to look away.

Emma closed the bathroom door and looked into the bag, setting an upturned box of cakes onto the vanity unit. She changed into new underwear and some joggers that Bella had given her. On her top half she wore a long-sleeved thermal top. She returned to the main room and put the box of cakes onto the worktop.

"You baked cakes in there?" he said. "That's impressive."

"What did you think I was doing?" she replied.

"Please, sit at the table," Leon said, with the proud swagger of a concierge. Cutlery had been set out, and ski magazines and crumpled piste maps were shunted at the other end. Emma took her seat and Leon carefully set a steaming plate of food in front of her. It was half a dozen fish fingers, arranged in a circle. Most of them were chopped in half and stood upright, with more fish fingers lain across the tops. Emma felt like she was five years old, as Leon hovered excitedly with a tea towel hanging from his arm.

"It's Stonehenge," he said. "Because you are from Britain."

"Oh!" Emma said. She smiled for the first time since that fateful moment earlier in the afternoon. She gently rotated the plate. "It's important that it faces north," she said.

Leon returned to the kitchen and opened the fridge. Masked by the chinking of glass bottles and his noisy rummaging for a bottle opener, Emma quietly picked up his cutlery and arranged it so that the handle of the knife and fork began at each end of a fish finger. She placed a second fish finger on top, sandwiching the cutlery in between. Leon returned with the two beers and looked curiously at her creation.

"Swiss Army Knife," she said. "Because you are from Switzerland."

He laughed from his belly and brushed the orange crumbs from his cutlery onto his thighs.

"They're good, huh?" he said.

"Hmmm," she said, closing her eyes to accentuate her mindful pleasure as she ate. "You're quite the chef."

After a long pause, he said "I'm sorry about today. That really sucks. Was he always like this?"

She sighed, setting down her knife and fork. Several fish fingers had been consumed, and many more had dominoed. It looked even more realistic.

"The Kendal I met was unrecognisable to the beast he is today," she said. "I was backpacking in Vietnam, and we met in a hostel. We hit it off immediately. It sickens me to say it, but he was fun and energetic, and smart. We travelled for a few days, and then parted ways because I was heading to Australia, and he was returning home."

Emma resumed her dinner. Leon, who had wolfed his down, sat back to allow Jas onto his lap, and tried in vain to stop her licking leftover crumbs from his plate.

"Then I was in Sydney. Two weeks later, guess who shows up at my hotel?" Emma said.

"If it's not Kendal, I want my money back," Leon said.

"Indeed. At the time, we had a lot in common. Both of us had finished degrees at stuffy old universities and were letting our hair down before starting careers. Surf lessons on Bondi. Karaoke till the sun came up. It was fun. He was fun."

Emma finished the last few sarsen stones and stacked her plate on top of Leon's.

"I'm sensing a *but*," Leon said.

"It turns out Kendal's rich, as you know. I didn't even know while we were travelling. I knew he wasn't poor, but when he invited me to meet his parents it was something out of *Game of Thrones*."

"They had a dragon?" Leon chuckled as he washed up the plates and baking sheet.

He brought the box of cakes to the table, slicing the tape with his thumbnail. Inside were four apple strudels dusted with icing sugar. They were a little battered from the journey, but Leon's eyes lit up nonetheless. He picked one up and ate it in one hamster-cheeked bite. Emma took another before it was too late.

"Worse. They had a maze."

Leon laughed so loud that Jas jumped down from his lap and slinked into the lounge.

He gazed across the room and muttered an impersonation of a Victorian duke; "I like the feeling of being *lost*. But not enough to leave the grounds. I need a maze."

Emma ate her cake and then closed the box.

"It was actually quite easy to get lost on Kendal's parent's estate. Anyway, him being rich was more of a curse than a blessing.

It became his *thing*, and the geeky guy I met in Asia disappeared. Thank God I kept my own flat. In that first summer, he cheated on me with a secretary from his work. We broke up, and then, fool that I am, I got back with him."

"And what made you go back to that bazillionaire?" Leon asked, baring his teeth in anticipation of her reaction.

"Very funny. It certainly wasn't his money. I have my own. The sad thing about Kendal is, somewhere inside there is a good guy. Or is there? I'm annoyed with him, but even more annoyed at myself. I always do this; try to fix things when I should just walk away."

Leon fed the stoves and Emma moved to a sofa, scooping up Jas and placing her in the groove where her thighs met.

"So what are you going to do now?"

Emma shrugged. "I don't know." She shook her head. "I can't think straight right now."

"You should get some sleep." Leon said. "We've got an early start tomorrow."

"We do?"

"Sure. Skiing at 9am, remember?"

"Erm, do I get a say in this?" she said.

"Skiing is life, Emma. You can't just sit there all day with a cat on your lap."

"I was going to go to town and book a flight out of here," she said.

"I understand. And your resignation is not accepted. So, I'll see you in the morning for strudel, coffee, and parallel turns."

Emma shook her head in exasperation, and pivoted so that her legs were up on the sofa and her head back on a cushion. She pulled a blanket over her. Leon returned, brushing his teeth.

"Do you want something to read?" he asked, head tipped back to prevent the toothpaste from spilling down his chin.

"Sure. What do you have?"

"Ski magazines ... but they're in German. Or Dickens," he said.

"Dickens?"

"Yes, Charles Dickens. You've not read Charles Dickens?" he asked.

"Of course. I just wasn't expecting that."

"So, you want one?" he said, spitting into the kitchen sink and washing it away.

"Because today couldn't get any weirder? " she asked. "No, I'm okay for Dickens. But thanks. Good night, Leon."

Chapter Thirteen

♥

"Good morning," Leon said, flicking on his gas stove and wiping the condensation from the kitchen window. He flipped open the cake box and gasped to see just one strudel remaining. Emma was at the dining table, already wearing her salopettes and ski socks.

"Woke up single and hungry," she shrugged. "What's a girl to do?"

Leon devoured the remaining cake in one gulp and slid two mugs from the cupboard. He wore his paprika snowboard pants, the cuff tattered from dragging on the floor. On his muscular torso he wore black and white plaid shirt, one sleeve rolled up to his forearm and the other unbuttoned and flapping around. Emma wanted to straighten them out and tuck his dark hair behind his ears so she could see his eyes.

"Jas slept on top of me all night," she said proudly.

"She was probably just cold," he replied.

Emma rolled her eyes.

"So, we're really doing this?" she said. "You're forcing me to go skiing against my will?"

"You specifically said you wanted to get really good, and that was just yesterday."

"That was when I wanted to ski with Charlie and Bella. Now I'd rather run them down than ski alongside them."

"You still need a lesson," he said. "Controlled attack requires skill."

"You would know," she said.

"Can you make the coffee?" he asked. "I have to check on my girls."

Leon pulled on a pair of boots which were rubberised up to the laces, as if he had trodden in deep puddles of tar. He opened the door, letting in a burst of cold, but blissfully fresh, air. Emma watched from the kitchen window as he trudged across the yard in front of the house to an outbuilding. She swallowed; her mind racing with ugly thoughts of Leon's collection of 'girls' locked up inside. Was she just the latest victim, to be dragged kicking and screaming into the shed? Would she kick and scream, she wondered, raising an eyebrow at her own inner monologue.

Emma noticed that the sputtering noise from the coffee percolator had stopped and she shut off the gas. She pinched the handle of the pot with a tea towel and poured a thick shot of espresso into each cup. Leon returned, walking snow into his kitchen.

"The girls?" she said, passing him a cup.

"They're okay. Cold, of course, but alive. Damn, this is strong," he said, grimacing at the bitter coffee. "Did you water it down?"

"No. Toughen up."

Leon grinned, but didn't accept the challenge. He added a drop of water, then downed it. Emma blew on hers, swilled it around the mug to cool it, then drank it undiluted with eyes squeezed so tight that tears formed in the corners.

"Delicious," she said.

He set off from the front door once more, this time with his ski jacket and backpack. Emma petted Jas one last time, then grabbed her goggles and mittens.

"Is it okay if I leave my bin liner of belongings here until I find a room or a flight?" she said.

"Of course," he said.

The sky was soft vanilla; cloudless and so bright that Leon put on his sunglasses and Emma added a pair to her mental shopping list. The yard in front of Leon's cabin had log stores stacked to their snow-covered roofs, and the unmistakable cluck of chickens.

"Your girls?" she asked.

Leon opened the wooden door to an outbuilding large enough to house a car, and Emma followed him in. She was taken back to her childhood immediately by the earthy smell of ammonia and chicken feed. A walkway cut through the middle of the building, straw scattered on the concrete floor and enough head height to stand comfortably. Under the eaves were deep wooden shelves, thick with straw and divided into box-like sections. Beams cut across the room like branches, which Leon ducked under slowly to avoid disturbing the roosting birds.

"Leon, your hen house is bigger than my flat," Emma said.

He reached into a shelf and stroked the tufted crown of a huge white speckled chicken. The bird seemed affectionate and curious but remained steadfastly buried in her nest of straw.

"This is Madame Defarge," he said. "She is the boss of the hen house."

He led Emma down the centre of the coup, careful not to crush the mounds of oats and peas. A few chickens were on the ground, pecking around his feet. Most were up high in their warm nests or perched on ladder-like horizontal planks. He reeled off more names.

"Clara, Flora, Nancy..."

At the far end was a cat flap at ground level, but snow had built up against the outside, layers of grey-blue visible through the plastic. Leon barged open the door to show off the chicken's outdoor area, enwrapped in wire mesh. He kicked a trench into the snow around the flap and bashed it until its frozen bonds broke and it swung free. They returned through the chicken coup and he scooped up a small, white chicken.

"Nell?" Emma said.

He looked at her with narrowed eyes, and gently placed the chicken back. Emma opened the door and slipped outside, careful not to be followed by a mischievous hen.

"How did you know her name?" Leon asked, pacing after her.

"Lucky guess," she called back. "Come on now, let's go to town."

Emma saw that the property had a driveway which snaked off into the forest but looked for now like a glacier. A vehicle was parked near the house, so thick with snow that she could only make out its oversize tyres wrapped loosely with chain. Leon led the way past it, onto a forest path. What had been terrifying and ominous last night now felt like something from a fairy tale. Emma sunk deep footprints into the snow, overtaking Leon so she could spot the tracks of animals that had come overnight.

"Leon, what's this?" she said, pointing to an unusual track which seemed to come in pairs, two large and two small.

He crouched over it and examined.

"Mountain hare," he said. "We get so many beautiful animals here. Marmots, chamois, golden eagles. We even have lynx."

"You do not have wild lynx," she said, more as a question than a statement.

"We do, but there's only one hundred and fifty in the whole of Switzerland. I've never even seen a footprint."

He resumed their trek along the path.

"Did I already say the name of my chicken?" he called back.

"They're all characters from Dickens books. Dickens chickens. I was waiting for a Little Nell, so when I saw the small one, I guessed it."

"Damn, you are a detective woman. No wonder you busted your boyfriend having sex with Alice."

"Thanks for that reminder, Leon," she said, hurling a messy snowball at his back.

The village looked stunning in its blanket of snow, as though a god-like pâtissier had piped icing onto every surface. The whole place glistened and sparkled as the low winter sun splashed light on icicle strewn rooftops. Leon waited on the bench outside while Emma fetched her skis and boots.

"Let me get us breakfast," she said. "I owe you for the Michelin-star fish finger dish you created last night. And everything else."

He kissed his fingertips, fanning them out like a firework. Over a breakfast of scrambled eggs and grilled tomato on dense, dark bread, Emma watched children sledge at the foot of a ski run.

"Leon, I've got lots of problems, as you know. I'm homeless. I've wasted two years of my life with an ass. I'm probably being fired. And I'm trying not to be mean Emma, but the thing that's stressing me out is my sledge. I brought a toboggan on holiday," she said.

"No problem. I rent sledges. I have dozens."

"This sledge is special."

"My sledges have steering wheels, so..." he said, like the biggest gangster in gangland.

"This isn't a competition. I'm just saying, mine has a lot of memories in it, and I need it back. It's at the chalet."

"So, ask Kendal," he said, eying up her second slice of bread. She dragged it toward her with a fork, then angled the blade of her knife so that he wouldn't risk a grab.

"It's like eating breakfast with a sea gull," she said. "Anyway, I can't go back there. I don't have a phone and I don't want to see him."

Leon sat back in his chair.

"Ok," he said.

She looked at him with a cute smile, waiting for him to catch up with her train of thoughts.

"Ah. No way," he said. "*Hi, I've got your girlfriend in my cabin. I've come for her sledge.* No. It's too weird."

"Says the man with a chicken called Little Nell," she said. "And also, I'm not his girlfriend."

"How about Alice?" Leon suggested. "She owes me a favour. She was the first woman I saved from certain death this week."

Emma stabbed a tomato, sending a spatter across her plate.

"No," she said firmly. "Alice would probably take it for a ride and smash it to pieces. She is not on our team."

Leon whistled quietly.

"That was great" Leon said, as Emma glided to a stop at the foot of a green run. "I just need you to lean more forward, so your shin is making contact with the front of your boot. Not resting weight on it, but so you can feel it."

She nodded, and the two of them shuffled toward the chair-lift. Emma leaned toward the sensor and the light flashed green, allowing the turnstile to rotate forward. She pushed on her poles and slid to the black line that marked the pickup point for the chairlift. Leon stood alongside her, with his backpack on his front so it would not get squashed by the seat back. The bench came swinging round and scooped them up, causing Emma to giggle.

"Do you think you'll always find chairlifts funny?" he said, as they were hauled up into the cool morning air.

She looked down at a conga line of kids, snaking messily down the slope beneath them.

"Do you not?" she said. "It feels like a gigantic baseball glove is lifting you into the sky. I don't think I'll get bored of the ski schools either. Their crash helmets are so huge; they look like mushrooms."

Leon chuckled. "My job is to keep them upright, but I *still* laugh every time they fall over. Especially when the front one falls and they all domino. Emma, you seem like you're in quite a good mood considering you caught your boyfriend..."

"Shh!" she snapped. "If I think about it, I get mad. Especially if I think about my job."

She made her lips into a small circle and exhaled slowly. Their uphill journey continued in quiet serenity. Emma swung her skis a little in an attempt to slice away a mound of snow on the tips. Their chair began to ascend a steeper section, with jagged tree stumps and rocky outcrops.

"Is this where I dropped my phone?" she asked.

He nodded.

"I think it is around there," Leon said. "To the left of that snow fence.

"Hmm, I think it was higher, up past that birch stump. Can you believe he was tracking me?" she asked. "Eager to get his grubby little hands on Alice. Checking he had plenty of time. Was he planning to clean the sheets before I got home?"

"I mean, Alice probably would have done that. That is her job," Leon said.

"Changing the beds. Not shagging the guests in them. Is she hoping for a massive tip?" Emma shuddered.

"Sounds like she had more than the tip," Leon muttered.

The chairlift approached the top of the escarpment and the duo lifted their skis from the foot rests, ready to dismount. Emma slid onto the gentle downslope and pushed herself out of the danger zone with her poles. She followed Leon to the top of a piste that descended into a huge, treeless bowl. It was a side of the mountain they had not yet explored.

"Leon, I am really enjoying my morning. And until the last five minutes, I managed not to think about Kendal and the fact I have to make a whole new set of friends in London. And that I have to sit next to him on the return flight, and so on. But I really need a phone. Is there a phone shop in the village? Or do you have an old one I could use to search for a hotel?"

"Emma, you're asking a man who has to tap a number button three times to get the letter L. But I could ask one of my friends if we can use their computer."

"That would be great. Is it absolutely out of the question that we could find mine?" she said.

He shook his head.

"I bet we could," she said.

"Emma, are you crazy? It would have been warm when you dropped it, so it would have burrowed down to the bottom of the snowpack. That could be a metre deep. And where exactly would we dig? And how could we get to that steep section?"

"Okay, okay," she said. "I didn't take you for a great big chicken. Let's ski."

He raised his eyebrows and they set off down a gentle green run that snaked back and forth around a vast, east-facing bowl. The sun warmed her cheeks, and Emma began to glide past another beginner who had no idea that he was in a race. She kept her skis parallel and whooshed past, then slammed on the brakes by skidding sideways, just making it round a tight bend. To her total surprise, Emma shot out of the turn and continued down the slope. Leon raced to catch up.

"Whoa Emma, that was perfect! Nice job."

Chapter Fourteen

♥

E mma passed a lunch menu to Leon, looking at her own reflection in his sunglasses.

"My shout," she said. "As you keep reminding me, you did rescue me last night. And we're celebrating. I am no longer the slowest person on the mountain."

Leon ordered a pizza Savoyarde, which had a topping of potato, cheese, and cream. An Alpine speciality which Emma decided was too much of a carb overload for her, even during a post-breakup grace period. She ordered a sensible Nicoise salad, which at least Leon would be unlikely to steal. They sat on a picnic bench on a busy deck area, where a constant flow of colourful snowboarders and skiers criss-crossed the salted wooden boards.

"I can see why you didn't want to go into the rental shop," Emma said.

He raised his eyebrows.

"Your employee, Chloe, has a cold, right?" she said.

"Yeah."

"I held my breath when I picked up my skis," Emma said.

"So, this afternoon, let's work on parallel turns," Leon said. "I know a great run over the back side, that gets the sun in the afternoon."

"I think I need to head down soon," Emma replied. "I have to do the tour of hotels to see what rooms are available. I'll try to find an internet cafe in town, although I think I might be ten years too late for that. Does the world still have internet cafes?"

"You know, you can stay at mine again," he said. "If you want."

She felt a flush of gratitude.

"I couldn't," she said. "It was so kind of you to rescue me last night, but I wouldn't want to impose. I need to get back to the city. I'll get a phone today and have my assistant book me flights home."

At the edge of the deck, hundreds of pairs of skis leaned against rows of metal racking, creating a messy fence. As Emma picked hers out, she heard someone shout her name. She swallowed hard when she saw Bella approaching in her black Armani one piece with fur trim. Emma cocked her head to the side to look beyond Bella.

"Are you okay?" Bella demanded, leaning over to give Emma a kiss on the cheek. "I've been calling, but Kendal said you lost your phone."

"Yes, I did. I'm fine."

Emma instinctively looked around for Leon, and spotted him waiting in the sun, flexing his skis.

"You know, you could come back to the chalet. Have you found a hotel?" Bella asked. "We've been worried."

Emma nodded. "I'm fine, Bella. I don't want to see him."

Bella pursed her lips.

"Look, Emma, it's really up to Kendal to say this, and not me. But he's heartbroken. He feels awful for what happened, and he's desperate to speak to you. To explain and fix it."

"Nope," Emma said.

"*Nope*?" Bella repeated.

"I don't want to hear from Kendal, ever again. What could he possibly say? I caught him in bed with another woman."

"But, accidents happen, Em."

Emma furrowed her brow. To hear it come from a woman felt even more ludicrous than hearing it from Kendal.

"Emma, this life that the guys give us," Bella said, raising her hand to indicate the mountain vista. "It takes a lot of pressure. They work hard. Sometimes they blow off a little steam, and yes, they make mistakes. But is it worth ending it all over one mistake?"

"So, you think 'boys will be boys', and I should accept that now and then he'll sleep with a stranger?"

Bella shrugged. "We all have our demons," she said.

"We don't all shag them," Emma said. "I'm going now. I've got a ski instructor waiting for me."

Bella watched Leon lean forward against the shins of his boots at an impossible angle, lifting the backs of his skis from the snow.

"Just wait a minute, Em. Hear what Kendal has to say."

"Bella, I've always liked you, and I will miss you. But I'm afraid you and I don't agree on this one. I've forgiven Kendal before, and I don't forgive *myself* for that. Never again."

Emma left Bella standing outside the restaurant and walked across the snowy plateau to Leon.

"I'm going to head down," she said. "I need to find a hotel for tonight."

"Okay. I will come down with you," Leon said.

The two of them boarded the gondola, which was otherwise empty. They sat opposite on bench seats and said little as it descended over the treetops. As it approached the village, she picked out Kendal's chalet from the window. Her eyes widened.

"Leon! I have an idea," she said. "What if we went to the chalet now? I know those three are up at the restaurant. Alice doesn't come until late afternoon. We could get my sledge."

"You want me to do a burglary with you?" he smirked.

"Yes. No. It's not a burglary because it's my chalet, technically. If we get caught, it's just that I've taken you back to my chalet."

"Do you have the key?" Leon asked.

She shook her head.

"No, but the boot room is normally left unlocked. That's where my sledge is."

"Sure. I'll do the robbery," he said. "In return for dinner."

"I might be back in London by then," Emma said.

"Then get it yourself," he said abruptly. "That's my fee."

"I'll leave you the money. Leon, I have to get back. I can't find a hotel, and my London life is hanging by a thread. I don't have a phone, nothing."

He shook his head.

"I don't want your money," he said.

The gondola clunked into the base building and the two of them disembarked onto the rubber matting. They trudged through a side street to the rental shop, skis and poles over their shoulders. Leon sat on a bench outside to remove his ski boots.

"Could you take these in, please?" he said. "My shoes are in the cubby hole behind the desk."

Emma held her breath and pushed open the door, returning a minute later with her and Leon's hiking boots.

They sat side by side on a bench and laced up their footwear. Emma got up first and reached out a hand to Leon.

"Come on," she said. "We've got a crime to commit."

They set off up the hill to Kendal's chalet.

· ♥ · ♥ · ♥ · ♥ · ♥ ·

Sure enough, the side door was open and Emma let herself in. She held it ajar, but Leon waited at the end of the path.

"Oh, come on, Leon! Don't tell me you're a great big chicken?"

"I thought I was on watch," he chuckled and followed her inside. The basement looked halfway between a garage and a sauna. The floor was concrete, with mesh covered drains to collect the snowmelt. The walls and built-in benches were clad in pine.

Emma's original set of skis remained in the corner where she had abandoned them the previous day, the poles hanging from the ski tips. Her sledge sat on the floor, and had been used as a table of sorts, with some gloves and mittens piled on it. She shoved them aside.

"Does it really take two people to steal a sledge?" Leon asked.

"I'm not stealing," she said. "It's mine, remember. Hold this!"

Emma lifted the toboggan by its wooden runners and thrust it toward Leon. He inspected it carefully, running his thumb along the steam-curved ash.

"This is beautiful," he said. Leon turned to leave, but Emma tried the door to the rest of the house and found it open. She looked at him with a grin.

"Go on then," he said. "I'll wait down here."

"No, come on!" she insisted. "Leave the sledge, let's go and be burglars. There's a list of stuff I forgot."

"Well, when you put it like that," he shrugged, setting the sledge back down on the concrete floor.

"Hellooo?" Emma shouted as she climbed the stairs. There was no answer, and she continued up to the second level where the bedrooms were.

"I need some things I left in the bathroom," she said.

Emma paused outside Kendal's bedroom door, and the excitement of the adventure evaporated. Her smile fell, and she looked to Leon for support. He reached for the handle and pushed it open. The bed was immaculately made up, with half a dozen throw pillows scattered against the headboard. One was a heart shape and said Mountain Life.

"It makes me feel sick," she said.

"Me too," Leon said. "I hate those stupid little pillows."

"Just turn around," she ordered, and he obeyed, allowing her to unzip his backpack and insert a bottle of conditioner and hair serum she had purchased on the first day at eye-watering expense. She also gathered up a pair of her ski socks which had been neatly folded and set onto a sideboard beside an ornamental jar of pebbles.

A door slammed downstairs and the two of them froze. Emma looked wide eyed in alarm. Before they even had time to think, they heard the thump of feet on stairs.

Emma dove onto the floor and pulled herself under the bed, hands scrabbling against the smooth wooden floorboards. The footsteps got louder, and Leon dropped into a press up position and swam in beside her. Emma pulled at his jacket, but Leon's backpack caught on the underside of the bed frame. The sound changed from the hollow creak of stairs to the solid thud as a foot met the landing.

Leon wriggled his arm free from the strap just as the bedroom door handle turned. Emma reached over him and yanked the bag under the bed, the sound masked by the opening door. They froze with her arm still wrapped around him and their faces just inches apart. They barely breathed, not least because the smell of Kendal's after shave made Emma feel nauseous. The slats bowed as Kendal sat heavily above them, and Emma watched him pull the long ski socks from his feet.

Kendal sniffed the air, and then reopened the bedroom door, stepping out onto the landing.

"Alice?" he called downstairs.

Emma rolled her eyes.

There was no answer, and he returned to the bedroom and into the ensuite. The bathroom door closed behind him and they heard the shower turn on. Leon waited a moment, listening carefully for the change in pitch that told him the water was hitting a body, and then crawled out from under the bed. Emma followed, and the two of them tiptoed across the room and down the stairs. They slipped back outside, with Emma carrying the sledge, arms threaded through the runners like a backpack. Leon led them down a path between two chalets, to get them off the main road.

Emma burst into laughter. She sat on her sledge and kicked her feet against the snow to move herself along.

"What next?" Leon said, cheerily. "Shall we rob a bank?"

"I would love to continue our crime caper, but I need to go on a tour of hotels," Emma replied. "I'll never get flights sorted, but at least I can get a room."

He nodded, and towed her back into town where she dropped off her belongings at the rental shop.

"I will wait at the bar and catch up with some friends," Leon said. "You can come and find me when you are ready. I hope you find somewhere."

Emma bared her teeth.

"Leon, I'm so sorry you've had to babysit me for days," she said. "I will get out of your hair as soon as I can, I promise."

"No, I didn't mean it like that," he said.

"It's okay. Fingers crossed," Emma said.

Chapter Fifteen

E mma washed her ski socks in the sink, foaming them into a lather with shampoo. She even added a drop of conditioner, since she figured they were having the toughest week of their lives. Leon had a washing machine, but Emma didn't want to impose any more than necessary.

She followed the thud of an axe and found Leon out the front, splitting wood in the last few rays of afternoon light.

The unbuckled straps on his dungarees swung from his waist as he methodically placed log after log onto the tree stump and blasted through them. He paused when he saw Emma and leaned on his axe, breath misting in the cold air. A bead of sweat ran down his jaw, dark with stubble, and he cocked his head to wipe it on his shoulder.

"Don't stop on my account," she smiled.

The cabin sat in a forest clearing with a frozen pond beyond the hen house. To the rhythmic thwump of the axe, Emma soaked up the vastness of the hazy-pink sky until her hands got uncomfortably cold.

Eager to muck in, she ran the water at the kitchen sink and filled a plastic bowl. The washing up bottle was empty, and she briefly looked under the sink, finding only rags, sponges, and bin liners.

"Is there any more washing up liquid?" she called from the kitchen window.

"Left hand door," Leon responded.

There were three doors at the back of the cabin. Leon's bedroom on the right, the bathroom in the middle, and a third one off the lounge. Emma opened that door, expecting a cupboard but finding something else entirely. A bedroom, decorated with warm, bold orange and yellow tones, which seemed out of kilter with the rest of the cabin. A chaise-longue with a cardigan and bra slung over it. A makeup table packed with bottles and jars, surrounding an ornate mirror. Emma listened for the thwack of the axe out front and entered the room. Unable to contain her curiosity, she opened the wardrobe and a heeled boot fell out. She stuffed it back beneath the hems of skirts and dresses and long winter coats. On top of the makeup table was a framed photograph of Leon with his arm around a beautiful woman. It was taken in summer, a selfie of the two of them with their heads almost touching and loving smiles on their faces.

Emma closed the door and returned to the kitchen, her mind racing. Roommate away on business? Ex-girlfriend too wounded to collect her stuff? Current girlfriend's dressing room? What did it matter, she reasoned. This wasn't a Kendal situation. Leon had never claimed to be single. He was a host and she was a grateful guest. Nothing more.

She washed up a couple of mugs with the dregs from the old washing up bottle. Leon came inside, his face rosy and flushed, his arms with a faint sheen of sweat. He crouched next to her and rooted around under the sink. She felt the heat from his body, and stepped aside so that he didn't touch her legs.

"Oh, I'm out," he said. "Sorry."

"Don't be sorry, you haven't done anything wrong," she smiled, but it came out nasally where she was trying to avoid breathing in his pheromones.

· ♥ · ♥ · ♥ · ♥ · ♥ ·

Leon lifted the lid from a simmering pan on the stove, filling the cabin with the aroma of red wine and beef. The smell of home-cooked food combined with the crackling log fire reminded Emma suddenly of the farmhouse.

The cabin's open plan interior was modern and tastefully decorated with hand-crafted wooden furniture, stacks of books and cosy-looking throws. The sofas faced each other, and Emma couldn't help but wonder who might emerge from the second bedroom.

"Leon, why don't you have a television?" she asked after a moment.

He instinctively looked at an angular cabinet in the corner of the lounge which held a lamp made of antlers. An oblong-shaped patch of varnish remained darker than its surround.

"I don't know. I'm saving up," he said.

"That's why you're skipping lunch. To save up for a television? Why don't I believe you?"

Leon brushed his hands on his thighs and crouched by a record player.

"I have music, though. Metallica or mostly classical."

"Binary options," she said. "Classical?"

He set some quiet orchestral music she didn't recognise and returned to the stove, cracking pepper into the stroganoff.

"Leon, I know we've only known each other for a couple of days, but we did a burglary together. We're partners in crime. You can be honest with me."

He raised his eyebrows. "Honestly, Emma. I have loads of metal and some old classical stuff that my parents left. Maybe Abba, if you can stomach that?"

"I meant the television," Emma said. Leon glanced back at the corner. "You and your girlfriend, or whoever, must want to watch TV in the evenings."

He raised his eyebrows.

"It's not a big deal," she said after his silence dragged on. "I don't care. None of my business."

Leon lowered the heat on the hob and put a lid onto the stroganoff. He pulled up a stool alongside Emma's and topped up their glasses.

"I'm not like him," he said. "I don't have a girlfriend."

She smiled. "I'm sorry. I know I'm being terribly nosey. I've got this lie detector in my mind right now and I'm paranoid, I suppose. I just want to know you're normal, and not about to murder me. We're roommates. I like to know who I am living with."

"That's a big leap from the missing television," he said.

"That was pretty fun, being under the bed today," he said, as he finished Emma's leftovers. "I felt like a kid."

"About that," Emma said with a grin.

She went to the coat hooks and retrieved a phone from her jacket pocket. She set it onto the table, her smile to the side and nervously biting her lower lip.

"You got a new phone?" Leon said.

"It's Kendal's," she admitted, baring her teeth in anticipation of his reaction. Leon shook his head but couldn't hide his smile.

"Emma! It's going to be so obvious you stole it. The two items that are missing are his phone and your sledge."

"I know, I know," Emma said, putting her head in her hands. "The thing is, I didn't *steal* it. I'm borrowing it."

"So you can find hotels, I suppose. You know you can stay here as long as you need to."

Leon said, topping up Emma's wine glass with a drop of merlot.

"This wine is really good," she said. "What is it?"

He looked at the label and placed it back on the worktop.

"Wine," he said. "Stop trying to change the subject."

"Oh yeah. So, I haven't turned it on because I want to save the battery. We don't have a charger. I have a plan, see. It involves you."

Leon sighed. "Go on then."

"You know how iPhones have Find My Phone?" she began.

"No."

"Well, they do. It shows a map, and it pinpoints where your friends' phones are. Well Kendal has my phone's location on his phone. That's how he 'knew' I was up the mountain when he was... Anyway. My plan is; you and I go to that spot under the chairlift where I dropped my phone, and we turn on Kendal's phone and pinpoint the location of my one. Dig a hole, get my phone back, boom. Then I'll post Kendal's phone through his letterbox. I'll say I picked it up by mistake."

"Emma, there are so many reasons why this plan cannot be done. It is crazy! When you post the phone back, isn't he going to realise that the only time you could have stolen it was while he was in the shower?"

"Yes, but who cares? He literally shagged the housekeeper in my bed. I'm not going to feel guilty for walking into what technically remains *my* bedroom."

"Okay. But the whole digging for buried treasure thing. I told you already; it can't be done. Tomorrow we should return Kendal's phone and be done with it."

Emma wiped her mouth with a napkin, calmly stood up and did an impression of a gutless velociraptor.

Chapter Sixteen

♥

E mma slid her telemark ski forward and felt it grip against the snow. It was a strange feeling after days of using downhill skis which slipped forward and back like roller skates. Using the purchase it gave her, she was able to thrust her left ski forward, and repeat the process. Within a few strokes, she found that she didn't even have to wait for one ski to stop before marching forward with the other. It was like power walking on a travelator, and she quickly caught up with Leon, whose head torch lit the path ahead.

"This is really fun!" she shouted. Her breath formed a mist, and her tongue felt the snap of cold. She shut her mouth and instinctively licked her lips, which she regretted immediately when they felt an icy sting.

"Enjoy the flat part," Leon said. "When it gets steep, it will be harder."

The base of the lifts felt otherworldly in the pre-dawn. Kiosks were battened down and the chairlifts hung motionless, piled with snow where there should be skiers. The thing that struck Emma most of all was the eerie silence. No mechanical whirring, no ski instructors tapping their poles above their heads. Just the occasional squawk of a chough, and the swoosh-swoosh of her skis shimmying through the snow in pursuit of her instructor. Leon set a path at the edge of the piste, in the last few feet of groomed corduroy before it fell away into ominous-looking woods.

The incline steepened, and Emma found herself having to lunge harder to make any progress. After twenty minutes, she stopped to tie her jacket around her waist. Looking down at the village, she felt a surge of pride at how far they had already ascended. Leon, who had already started up the next slope, looked back at her.

"Are you okay?" he shouted.

"I'm on top of the world," she shouted, harnessing her inner Kate Winslet.

"Not yet, you're not," he said.

She had awoken to Leon looming above her in the pitch-black lounge. It sent a jolt of panic through her and she yanked the blanket to her chin. He explained that they were going to look for her phone. Sidelights came on and the adrenaline subsided. With a hard-boiled egg in her pocket, they were out of the door at 5am. It was too early to ask questions, and she just followed Leon into the wilderness with skis over her shoulder.

They continued their exhausting ascent until Emma's quads burned like fire. She had to lay in the snow at one point to cool down. As the sky began to turn a pale indigo, they began to see other people for the first time. A snowmobile passed them, headlight shining in their faces as the ski patrol checked they were okay, before zooming off into the distance. A noisy grooming machine put the finishing touches to a perfectly combed ski run.

Leon paused at the base of a particularly steep hill, its surface covered with moguls. It looked grey-blue in the low morning light, like a stormy ocean had been frozen and upended to an impossible angle. To the right of the snowy slope was a steep pitch, peppered with rocks and trees but dominated by a metal tower that held a cable in outstretched arms. They leaned against their ski poles and caught their breath.

"Is that the lift?" Emma gulped.

"Yes. We have to go up this run, and then take off our skis and hike into the trees. I will tie you to me, so if you fall, I can catch you."

She nodded, feeling slightly bad for cajoling Leon into this mission by doing a chicken impression the night before. It suddenly felt much more serious than the treasure hunt she'd imagined.

Leon took a rope from his backpack and reached around her, passing the end from one hand to another. He leaned into her, his head brushing against her chest, and she felt the heat from his neck. He tied a loose knot in front of her hips and looped the other end around his own torso.

"You first," he said. "Then I can brace myself if you fall."

"Okay. And what should I do if *you* fall?" she asked.

"Well, the best scenario is that we slide back down to here, uninjured."

Emma didn't enquire as to what the worst scenario was, and instead began her assault on the steep mogul field. It was punishing work, but she eventually made it three quarters of the way up. Leon sat beside her and carefully unclipped the buckles around her boots. The telemark skis were narrower than the downhill ones she had used previously and had a length of fabric on the bottom to grip the snow.

"How come you have a girl's pair of touring boots?" Emma asked.

"I have a rental shop, remember?" he said.

"Right, but they were at your house. So, if this girl skied to your cabin, how did she get home?" Emma said with a teasing look.

Leon didn't answer. He dug their skis vertically into an icy mogul and set off into the scrub to the side. Emma followed in his footsteps, her legs disappearing to the knee.

"We have about twenty minutes until the lifts start up," he said. "Can you fire up Kendal's phone?"

She did so and was relieved that he hadn't changed his password. They huddled around the bright screen, and after a few nerve-wracking seconds of a blue dot lurching around the map, it homed in on a spot just downhill. Emma led the way, gripping stumps of trees to steady herself as she sank deep into the crystalline hardpack.

"It's saying my phone is here," she said.

Leon took a small avalanche shovel from his backpack and passed it to Emma, who began to dig. After some time, she hit rock and chipped away at the edges of the hole, digging out an area as big as a dustbin. Leon held the torch, which illuminated a dirty mixture of soil and snow, but no phone.

A mechanical groan came from one of the huge metal towers and the chairlift crept into life. A cluster of icicles dropped from the cable, silently piercing holes in untouched snow a couple of feet from their excavation.

"We have to go," Leon said. "The lifts are running."

"We're not directly under the lift," Emma pointed out.

She took the shovel and began to enlarge the hole where the ice had fallen, slicing down at its sides, and flinging shovels of icy debris downslope.

"Wait!" said Leon. "I think I saw it."

Emma peered into the hole.

"No, something flew out of the snow you dug out," he said, clambering down. Leon sifted through a pile of debris and picked out a black rectangle, brushing water from its face.

"Yesss!!" Emma shouted. She threw her arms around Leon without thinking and felt the rumble in his chest as he chuckled, holding her against him as he returned the hug.

The sun hauled itself above the jagged skyline as Emma and Leon made it to the top of the mountain. A journey that would have breezed by in just seven minutes on the gondola had taken them almost three hours. Emma unhooked her skis and leaned them on a ski rack, staggering towards the restaurant. An employee setting out deck chairs looked at her watch.

"First lift?" she asked.

"We skied up," Emma said proudly.

"Wow. Coffee?" the lady asked.

"That would be wonderful, thank you."

Emma and Leon oriented their deck chairs to watch the sun rise. They sipped their tiny Swiss coffees and ordered pancakes so that they would be first in line when the chef arrived. The sun splashed over Emma's face and she positively glowed. With her eyes shut, she reached a hand out and felt for Leon's arm.

"Leon, thank you so much for dragging me up here today," she said. After a long pause, she added "I really thought you were going to bottle it. And then this morning, when you woke me up, I didn't know what you wanted."

He laughed.

"Emma, you are the funnest girl that's ever stayed in my cabin. That's for sure."

"What about the one you buried in your garden? The one whose boots I'm wearing."

He snorted like a bull, and she thought it was a laugh, but he pulled himself out of his chair and walked in the direction of the lift. Emma sat up and shielded the sun from her eyes, watching him yank his skis from the rack and kick them on.

"Leon?" She called after him. When he didn't answer she climbed out of her deck chair and jogged over, as best she could in ski boots. By the time she reached him, he was flipping the buckle shut at the heel of his boot and skating off.

"Leon, I was joking," she said. "What's wrong?"

She watched, bewildered, as he slid over the knuckle of a ski run and disappeared out of sight.

By the time pancakes arrived, she realised he wasn't coming back. Repeating the comment in her mind, she couldn't understand why he had got so upset. She thought back to all the outrageous things *he* had said, like calling her Mean Emma the first day he met her. This was drama she didn't need.

She ate his pancake and decided to go to town for a phone charger.

Chapter Seventeen

"You're Chloe, right?" Emma asked.

The lady looked round, and Emma noticed her red nose and bloodshot eyes.

"Yes," she said. "But keep your distance, I have a cold. Have you seen Leon?"

Emma stepped back. She leaned the skis that she had used that morning onto a rack.

"I was with him until half an hour ago. Then he skied off and I haven't seen him since. These are his skis. These are his ski boots I'm wearing, too, but I have nothing to change into. My hiking boots are at his cabin."

Chloe raised her eyebrows.

"It's not like that," Emma said. "I just needed a place to stay. Long story. Chloe, shouldn't you be at home recovering?"

"I have ten people booked in today to pick up their skis, and if I go home then their holiday is ruined." Chloe croaked before blowing her nose loudly.

"Do you have a phone charger?" Emma asked.

Chloe lifted a wire from behind the counter.

Emma plugged her phone in, hesitating before she asked another question. "Can I help while I'm here? You look like you could use a break."

Chloe looked like she was about to cry. "Would you??

"I have set the skis up as best I can for their heights and weights, but I might need to make adjustments when they get here. If you get their boots done, then call me and I can come and make sure the settings are good. I live just up the street."

Chloe gave Emma a whistle-stop tour of the shop, showing her where to find all the different sized boots and poles. There was a simple paper system for matching the renter's details with the number on the tips of the skis. While Chloe put on her coat and gathered her belongings, Emma plugged in her phone and sat on a bench, leaning back against the wall to find it spiky. Behind her was a mountainscape mural, painted directly onto the wall in thick globules of paint.

"This is cool," she said. "Your work?"

"No. Sophie did it. You are a lifesaver. You have my number, just call me when you need something."

"Who is Sophie?"

"Leon's sister." Chloe said over her shoulder as she headed for the door.

"Does she still live with him? Where is she this week?" Emma asked.

Chloe lost what little colour she had in her cheeks, and returned to the shop, the door closing behind her.

"She passed away last winter. Has Leon not talked about it?"

"No."

"This was her shop. That's why he doesn't step foot in here anymore."

Emma stood frozen on the spot, rewinding various conversations she had with Leon. "Oh gosh. I had no idea."

"I'm not surprised. Leon never speaks of it, even to me," Chloe said.

She left, and Emma wedged the door open until she was confident that the place was aerated.

One or two groups came in to pick up their skis and deposit their trainers, but to Emma's relief, nobody needed fitting. For most of the morning she sat on a bench calling round every hotel in town, to a procession of mild chuckles. One particularly stuffy receptionist said they were taking bookings two years out for this half-term week. She called Swiss Air and put herself on a standby list but was warned not to expect much.

"Anthony, how are you?" she said once she got through to her assistant.

"I'm fine. Rather busy though. I've been loaned to Myriam."

"Oh," Emma said.

"Yes, Nigel said you were out of action, and that I could be a shared resource," Anthony said. "So, I'm printing contracts now."

"I've been gone 48 hours," Emma said. "Have I still got a desk?"

"Yes, but Davis has taken it. He thought you wouldn't mind, if you're away, and it's got a better view. It's all hands on deck, trying to win this Swiss client."

"I know, I know," Emma said, biting her nails for the first time in months. "I can do it, it's just..."

She noticed a figure at the window and immediately recognised the blond sweep of Kendal's hair, his blue eyes peering through the glass. The cowbell hanging above the door rang as he came in. Emma swallowed and stood up behind the counter.

"I've got to go," she said, hanging up the call.

"Emma," Kendal said, lips straight and serious. "What the devil are you doing in this ski shop?"

She ignored his question and remained somewhat protected by the wooden counter in the middle of the store. He held out a bunch of flowers, but she kept her arms crossed and eventually Kendal set them on top of some piste maps.

"Nice flowers. I'm sure Alice will love them."

"Emma, I am sorry about what happened," he said. "It was an accident. Really."

There was a pause as Emma processed his fumbled apology. She barely heard the word sorry, focusing on the word *it*. Not me or I, but *it*. The *Accident*. The thing that *happened*. Kendal was so passive in this recollection of the events. The victim, almost. His infidelity was not a choice, but a cold he had picked up that ruined everyone's holiday.

"Yes, the ice can be so dangerous, Kendal. Did you slip and fall up a flight of stairs and land on her?"

Emma produced his smartphone from her pocket as she spoke, pushing it across the counter with the tip of her finger, as if she had retrieved it from the depths of a festival toilet. Kendal snatched it up and pressed the power button to light it up and ensure it was his. Emma couldn't help but glance at the screensaver, a photo of Kendal with a beloved white Lamborghini he borrowed for a weekend. She shuddered at those look-at-me doors that swung skyward like dumb erections. The embarrassment of extricating herself from the cabin to grab a Double Decker, then having to loiter by the magazines until a crowd of strangers have finished taking their snaps.

"When did you get my phone?" he said. "Was I in the shower?"

"It got picked up accidentally when I was grabbing a few of my things," she said, in a line she had rehearsed in her head. Passive.

Kendal pocketed his phone. He stared at her for a moment, and tried a thin-lipped smile, which fell quickly.

"So, that's it? Is there nothing I can say?" he said.

"No, Kendal. There's nothing you can say."

"You know you can stay in the chalet. I am happy to sleep in the lounge. You really don't need to be working in a ski shop."

"I'm fine, Kendal. I have friends to stay with," Emma said. Behind the forced smile, she wondered if Leon was still speaking to her after she said he was a killer. Where would she sleep tonight? She could get the train down to a city, she thought. But first, she needed shoes. It was a maddening maelstrom of problems.

The door chimed, and a lady clattered in with a bundle of skis and two kids in tow. Kendal took his cue to leave, and Emma breathed a sigh of relief as he exited the building, and she hoped, her life.

At lunch time, there was a knock at the door, and a grin spread across Emma's face when she saw Leon was smiling. She ran over in her well-worn ski socks and stepped outside into the warm sun.

"Hello stranger," he said, passing her a paper package.

"Hey. Did you get my message?" she asked.

"Yes, yes," he said. "Don't worry."

They sat on a wooden bench, which had weathered to a silver grey. Emma unwrapped her panini and bit into it.

"Hmm. Leon, I'm sorry I said you were a psycho killer. That joke wore thin, I know."

"It's okay, Emma. I'm sorry I went off in a huff. I'm having a tough week."

"Oh," Emma said, suddenly feeling like a tremendous burden.

"No, not you. You've been the best part of my week. And today you have saved the day at this store, which I really appreciate. I just have money issues I have to deal with. It is putting me on edge."

They ate quietly, watching a brave snowfinch hop closer and closer to their crumbs.

"It probably doesn't help that I'm taking up all of your time. I must pay you for this morning. That was really magical, watching the sun come up. I can't believe we skied all that way!"

Leon shook his head.

"Don't pay me for that. It will take away something special. No. This is not a problem I can solve by giving ski lessons, sadly."

He tipped out the last of the crumbs for the bird, then screwed up the paper and tossed it into a bin.

"Are we skiing this afternoon?" he asked.

Emma shook her head.

"I can barely walk. Anyway, I have to work. Unless you want to take over?"

"Sucks to be you," he laughed. "What time do you get off?"

"What?" she said. "It's *your* shop. I'm on holiday. Why aren't you working while I go skiing?"

He swung his skis onto his shoulder.

"You can barely walk," he said. "Remember? I'll pick you up at five."

Emma learned that a ski rental shop was expected to do much more than simply rent skis. She tightened up enough snowboard bindings that by late afternoon she knew which size screwdriver to grab as they entered the shop. She carefully freed a zip that had cocooned a young girl in her one-piece ski suit. When it was time to actually rent skis, she found it relatively straightforward to fit the boots, and called in Chloe to set up the bindings out front.

It was so busy that she barely had time to look at her emails and felt better for it. Normally, being sidelined at her job would have crushed her, but she had more immediate concerns that pushed the career panic to the standby list. She was living out of a bin liner, sleeping on a stranger's couch, and dreading returning to London. Now that she had split up with Kendal, the network of friends they had built up would be cleaved in two.

She did message her mum. Emma had been sending updates every day for years, as routinely as she drank coffee in the morning and had an existential crisis at 3am. It kept her sane, even though she considered it so embarrassingly crazy that she had hidden it from Kendal throughout their relationship. She sent a picture of Jas, with the caption;

'Leon's cat. He took her in as a stray, so we have that in common x'

At five-o-clock she flipped the sign closed and turned off the lights. Leon came by to lock the door, and suggested they telemark home because it would be quicker than walking in boots. Emma, somewhat of an expert after her pre-dawn introduction, skied alongside Leon over pavements thick with snow.

"How was your afternoon?" she asked.

"I had a lesson."

"You don't need lessons," she said, in a joke straight from her father's playbook.

"Very funny. I gave a lesson to a couple who wanted to improve their turns. I guess that's what skiing is, improving turns. Is there anything else?"

"You tell me. Do you wish someone would ask for a lesson in how to go perfectly straight?" she said.

"Oh yes, that is my dream, Emma! I would take them to the very top of the mountain, and we point our skis, like this. Then BANG! Like a bullet from a gun."

He took a few powerful lunges and then tucked into a schuss position, gliding past the front of a little supermarket and down a snowbank alongside a flight of stairs. Emma held her breath until he reappeared on the pavement ahead of her.

"Yeeee haaaa! To the bottom. Three minutes later I am in the village on my way to the bar. Best lesson ever."

Emma giggled. "You got really into that one," she said. "Tomorrow, I'll do it. You might have to blindfold me, so I'm not scared."

"Emma, it will be one hundred times scarier if you can't see where you're going. But okay. I tied you to a tree on our last lesson. Next I will blindfold you."

She raised her eyebrows but said nothing. She had sworn herself off making serial killer jokes about him. The two of them skied along the road, a paper bag swinging from Leon's gloved hand.

Emma marvelled at a distant peak, its pistes blushed apricot by the setting sun. The mountains took on wildly different personalities as the light changed. Snow falling past amber streetlamps took Emma to Narnia. As they left the lights of town, the forests took on an ominous, fairy tale darkness.

"What's in the bag?" she asked.

"Dinner for two. Fine wine."

She laughed. "Don't tell me; is it red?"

"No, I thought I'd surprise you tonight. It's white, because we are having fish."

"Ooh. I love fish. What fish?" she asked.

"I don't know. Fish. You are so fussy, Emma. Types of wine. Types of fish. It's just the white fish like you get in fish fingers."

"As long as it's in the shape of an ancient monument, I'll be happy," she said.

"I got two bottles, so it might not be the night for balancing food. Maybe a pyramid. We'll see. Emma, what day do you go home?"

She felt a pang of sadness at the thought of London. Suddenly she was back in her flat, puncturing the film of a microwave meal and plugging away at her laptop until midnight.

"We have the late flight on Monday," she said. "I tried to change it today, so I wouldn't have to sit next to Kendal. But all the flights back to London are full, and my only option is an upgrade."

"Did you do it?" Leon asked.

"No. It was insanely expensive. And as much as I hate him, I'm not going to pay that much to get away from him. I'll just swap with Bella and sit on the other side of the aisle. Why do you ask? Wondering when you can have your life back?" she asked.

"I love having you to stay, Emma."

They took a different, longer route home along the roads, since the forest path was too bumpy. Leon slowed to ski alongside Emma.

"Emma, I wasn't entirely honest with you yesterday," he said.

She braced for the worst. "I lost my parents when I was in my late teens, and me and my sister moved into the cabin."

"Sophie?" Emma asked.

He cleared his throat and slowed to a pained crawl. Emma hung back to stay alongside him.

"She passed away just over a year ago. I find it hard to talk about."

"Leon, I'm so sorry," Emma said. They were down to a walking pace, piecing fresh tracks in the middle of a winding road which sliced through a deep forest. The snow looked blue in the fading evening light. Birds fluttered into the trees, preparing to roost for the cold night ahead.

She looked down at her skis, and swallowed.

"Leon, when I made the joke this morning about these boots, I had no idea."

He waved it away, looking at her with his cerulean eyes.

"I know. It struck a nerve but it wasn't your fault."

"I feel awful," she said, hand on heart.

"Please, if you knew Sophie, you would know she would be laughing about it."

Emma nodded, and the two of them continued their ascent of the winding road to Leon's cabin.

"The television," Leon said. "We were watching Friends one evening and Sophie got some paper and a pen. Started scribbling. I said what are you doing? Eventually she said 'four years'."

He smiled, warmth returning to his face as he relived the moment with his sister. Emma cocked her head to the side, curiously.

"She explained that if we watch two hours of television each night, for the next fifty years, that's four years of life spent watching television."

"Is that true?" Emma asked.

"Sophie was pretty good at maths, so I guess so. That was it, we turned it off and buried it in the yard."

"You buried it?"

Leon laughed..

"Yeah. We needed something to do. It was kind of boring once we turned it off."

"She sounds fun," Emma said. "I'm sorry to make you dredge up memories. I'm too nosey."

"It's fine," Leon said, his gaze on his path ahead. "It was a good memory. But it makes me sad to think about that scrap of paper. She never got her fifty years."

Chapter Eighteen

♥

T he cabin was unexpectedly warm when Emma stepped inside. Orange flames licked against the glass on both stoves.

"Have you been home already?" she said. "I thought you came straight from the slopes."

Leon put the wine and food into the fridge and stepped toward Emma by the front door. He placed a hand on hers, to pause the unzipping of her jacket. She cocked her head to the side in confusion, and Leon gently pulled her hat over her chestnut hair. He led her back outside.

"Where are we going?" she asked.

"Yes," he said.

The cabin was encircled by a veranda, stacked with logs, and protected from the weather by the wide overhanging roof. Instead of taking the steps down toward the front yard, Leon followed the deck around the building. It was much deeper than Emma had imagined, having only seen the main rectangular room at the front. As they approached the rear of the property, Leon turned to her and gently tugged her beanie down over her eyes. He took her hands in his, and she giggled nervously as she inched across the wooden boards.

"Okay, are you ready?" he said.

She inhaled, to calm her nerves, and found herself intoxicated by the fresh mountain air, the homely waft of smoke, and faintly, Leon's masculine smell. He lifted the brim of her hat back onto her forehead, and she immediately craned her neck to look past him.

Behind his cabin was a forest clearing about the size of a tennis court, which started level and then steeply sloped upward. At its edges were a dozen torches, staked into the ground and burning proudly against the dark woods beyond. Leon picked up her sledge and dragged it down the steps. Emma remained on the deck, taking it in, trying to imagine Leon rushing back after his lesson to stab torches into the ground.

"Come on," he said. "Let's see what you've got."

She scrambled up the hill behind him. As they neared the top of the run, it was steep enough that she had to put her toes into the steps that his boots had created. She sat at the top, momentarily exhausted by the climb. The cabin looked beautiful, a warm glow beckoning from its windows and wisps of smoke rising into the starry sky.

He sat on the sledge, and shimmied forward so there was room behind him.

"Really?" she said, looking down at the cabin. "Aren't we going to smash into the house?"

He laughed. "I didn't picture you for a great big chicken," he said.

Emma climbed on, feeling an electric rush of endorphins as she edged into Leon. She reached around him and squeezed his body, nestling her head into the crook of his shoulder. Her cheek touched his neck, and she felt his skin against her lips. Without a thought, she kissed him, as if it were the only natural thing to do. Emma opened her eyes and turned her head a little, hoping he hadn't noticed the soft touch of her lips against his jaw. He turned his face, stubble brushing against her cheeks – rosy with embarrassment. A wisp of his brown hair crept from his hat and his eyes smouldered with the reflection of the flaming torches. He licked his lips and swallowed, electrifying her.

"Are you ready for this?" he said, so gently.

She nodded and closed her eyes.

Suddenly, they lurched forward as Leon kicked at the snow. He scooped up her legs so she could not slow down the sled, and Emma gripped him once again so tight she thought she might break a rib. She screamed with alarm as the sledge accelerated over the knuckle and began hurtling toward the house.

"Stop! LEON!!" she shouted.

The cold night air and glassy fragments of ice blasted their faces as the toboggan raced downslope. Emma's pleading became a continuous scream, joined by Leon's guttural cackle. She had to close her eyes as the prospect of face planting into the cabin became a reality. The sledge whizzed across the flat section at the foot of the garden and ploughed into the stairs, which it managed to partially climb before slipping and tipping the two of them onto the ground.

Leon laughed. Emma reached over to thump him, but in her dazed state she missed, which made Leon laugh even louder.

"Is this where you point out some constellations?" she said, staring at the clear night sky.

"Maybe later," he said, rolling over and brushing the hair from her cheek with his thumb.

He moved toward her, and she felt a tremor of electricity at the thought of his lips meeting hers. But that buzzing, she realised, was coming from her pocket. She snapped her head to look down, causing their noses to knock against each other. He laughed it off as she unzipped her pocket.

"I'm sorry," she said, fumbling her gloves off to answer it. "It might be work."

Leon clambered off, his smile neutral and gamely. As she brought the phone to her ear, he scooped up the reins of the toboggan and jogged up the hill on his own, dragging it behind him like an unwilling Labrador.

Within two words, Emma knew it was a sales call and hung up, cursing herself for answering it. Leon stood on the summit and beat his chest like King Kong. He hurtled down the slope head-first with a huge grin on his face. Emma had to cover her eyes, and as her palm touched her nose, she wondered if the near miss had happened, or she had imagined it.

Leon's fish dinner was a non-event, but the wine went down like a toboggan on ice. When it got too cold to sit on the swing bench out back, they moved to the fireside couch, legs entangled on a neutral middle cushion.

"I am so glad I lugged that sledge across Europe," Emma mused. "It was beautiful out there tonight."

"I learned to ski on that hill," Leon said. "When I was three."

"Were you brought up here, in this cabin?" Emma asked.

"Kind of. My mother and father bought this plot of land when we were babies and built it. At the time, there were only one or two lifts, and it was a small hill for locals. We sledged and skied, and in the summer we would hike and fish."

"Sounds pretty idyllic," she said, wistfully. "My childhood was all outside, too."

"I can't imagine living anywhere else," he said.

"Well, it's a good job you don't have to. Speaking of jobs; can you believe I worked in your shop today? Is that even legal?"

He smirked.

"You're a lawyer, right? You should know," he said. "But yes, I can believe it. You can do anything, Emma. Hike a mountain, run a shop, rob a house. What exactly do you do in London? I don't know much about your job; only that your boss is a dick."

"Don't ask," she said, draining the last of her drink.

He scooped up Jasmine the cat and tickled her face. She purred like a drill.

"Corporate law," Emma admitted, eventually. She raised her head up to meet his gaze.

"That's cool," he replied.

"*Cool,*" she said. "Says the ski instructor."

"Yeah, why not? Isn't it one of those jobs that takes years of study? It does here in Switzerland."

Emma reached her hands around Jasmine and scooped her from Leon's lap. He sniggered as reluctant claws pulled at his jeans. Eventually Emma's theft was complete and the cat settled lazily on her thighs.

"It took seven years," Emma sighed, her voice heavy, more ashamed than proud.

"Why do you say that like you were in jail?"

"Because I was, basically. My whole adult life has been reading contracts. I thought law would be fighting for justice. Going to court and coming up with ingenious arguments to catch the bad guys."

"Wait, it's not?" he said.

The cat was now on her back, front paws folded like a mantis and seeming to smile as Emma ruffled the pepper grey fur on her belly.

"I think for some lawyers, there's the rough and tumble excitement of the courts. But I must have taken a wrong turn somewhere because all I seem to do is read small print which was designed to never be read. And worse, I write more of it."

"Right, but presumably you have a magnifying glass and a gun?" he said.

She screwed up her face.

"I'm not a detective, Leon. No."

"Do you at least have a wig and a hammer thing?"

Emma thought for a moment, her tongue pressing on the inside of her cheek. Then she recoiled at a memory.

"I have a hammer in the tool box under my sink. Not a gavel. And no wig either, because I'm not a courtroom lawyer or judge."

"So why did you make a face like you swallowed a wasp?" he asked.

She sighed.

"I know you've had enough of hearing about my ex, but I just remembered a time when he bought me a wig. And it was long black hair, exactly like his best friend's girlfriend. Funny, that.""Did you do her voice, and everything?"

Emma swung a cushion at Leon's head, the commotion causing Jasmine to leap from the couch.

"How did a farm girl end up working for *the man*?" he asked.

Emma forced a smile, but looked sadly at Leon.

"My mum always wanted more for me than village life. At a time when my parents had nothing, she spent what little they had to put me through a posh school. I suppose I had my dad's work ethic and my mum's ambition."

Leon nodded and looked at the fire, charred logs white with heat. His hand rested on Emma's tired thigh. He opened the log burner and fed it, the door creaking loudly as it closed.

"Village life is not so bad," he muttered.

"Oh, Leon I didn't mean that," she said, sitting up.

"It's okay," he smiled. "I also wonder what my mother would have made of me being just a ski instructor. She would be unsurprised, that is for sure."

Emma sat up, and took his hand to get his full attention.

"Your parents would be so proud of you, Leon. You're one of the kindest, most inspiring people I have ever met. You are so much more than *just* a ski instructor. I just wonder sometimes if I've gone down a rabbit hole I can't get out of."

"You're pretty fun when you're not trying to work at the same time."

"Today, I didn't do any work at all," Emma said proudly. "I worked in the ski shop, but that was fun. I mean, lawyer work. I had a couple of calls, but that's it. I can't remember the last day I took off, weekends included."

Emma rested her head on the soft couch, looking up at the log beams which criss-crossed the ceiling. Her face carried a look of genuine bliss.

"You took a day off, Emma," Leon said, giving her a pat on the leg. "Tomorrow, I will give you a little gold medal we normally save for kids when they get up from a bad slam. Except, you did take that call outside at 8pm. Maybe silver."

Leon tidied away a few bowls from the lounge and rinsed their wine glasses. She heard the bathroom door close and yawned.

Emma pinged a photo of the torchlit ski slope to her mum, adding a heart emoji. She reached across to put her phone on the coffee table but could only get the very corner onto the wooden surface. She gave it a flick, but it tumbled to the rug. Leon laughed, and she realised he had been watching her from the bedroom doorway. He looked handsome when he smiled, even as he wiped toothpaste from his chin. His torso was defined and muscular, but not overly so. A v-neck white T-shirt clung to his chest. His jeans hung low on his waist, belt undone as if he had begun getting undressed and then remembered he had company.

They looked at each other across the room.

"Emma, I was thinking..." he began, back against the door frame. The pause hung in the air as he gathered his thoughts.

"It was a tiring day, right?" she said, propping herself up on the couch.

"Exactly. We climbed a mountain before we'd had our second coffee," he said.

"And I started a new job," she added.

He ran his hand through his hair, which after a day inside his hat had become matted into spiky tendrils.

"Why don't you take my bed tonight, and I'll take the sofa?"

Why don't you take me to your bed? Emma thought before she could stop herself.

"I'm fine here," she said with a smile. "I can barely move. You just have to come and tuck me in and read me some Dickens."

"Deal."

The whirr of an electric toothbrush and the sight of herself in the mirror sobered her up enough that she felt self-conscious in knickers and a t-shirt. She opened the bathroom door and made a dash for the sofa while Leon checked on his hens. Emma was almost asleep when he returned. A draft of cold air crept into the lounge as he stamped snow from his boots, and Emma pulled the blanket up to her nose. Leon leaned over the back of the couch, kissing her on the forehead.

"How is Madame Defarge?" she asked, barely able to keep her eyes open.

"She's okay, but a fox has been at the coup. Some snow and dirt have been scratched up around the fencing. I leaned some wood against it for tonight, but I have to fix it tomorrow."

He pondered by a bookshelf, then pulled out a copy of *A Tale of Two Cities*. Emma laughed.

"Are you really doing this?" she asked.

"Of course. Chapter one. It was the best of times; it was the worst of times."

"Good night, Leon," Emma said.

He snapped the book shut and kissed her cheek, his lips lingering on her sun-blushed skin.

"Good night, Emma," he whispered before leaving. She smiled and sank deeper into his soft couch. Thoughts of magical forests, the soft purr of a cat, the crackle and pop of embers.

Within minutes Emma had fallen into the most blissful sleep of her adult life.

Chapter Nineteen

In a cafe at the edge of the town square Leon hung his jacket on the back of a chair. As he did so, his face brushed its lining and he jerked his head back.

"I need to wash my jacket," he said.

"When did you last do it?" Emma asked, grinning at him over the table

His pupils rose to the tops of his eyes and he counted up on his fingers. He stopped at three.

"Weeks or months?" she asked, bracing for the worst.

"Seasons."

She winced.

"Today we work on speed, Emma. Speed. Remember the toboggan? Remember the rush?!"

"How could I forget you lifting my feet up so I couldn't brake? That's your modus operandi, Leon. That fine line where romance becomes abuse."

She paused a beat and grabbed his hand on the table. "I don't mean it. Don't run off in a huff," she added.

He smiled and raised his eyebrows. Their crepes arrived. His with Nutella, hers with blueberries. The waitress asked Leon if he had any eggs, and he promised her soon.

"In what world does the waitress ask the customer for eggs?" Emma asked, letting go of Leon's hand to focus on her food.

"Do you have a thing that measures your speed?" he said. "Some of my clients have a watch, or a thing on their phone."

Emma gathered her thoughts, and thumbed through her phone until she located an app she had downloaded for jogging. Her history had a lonely lap of a south London park, which apparently took her sixteen minutes. The problem was, getting to and from the park had added precious minutes. And what if it rained? Instead she had bought a cycling machine for her living room, which remained boxed and became a sideboard for legal documents.

"I have one," she said. "But I am terrified of getting my phone out on the mountain. I have visions of it tobogganing down without me, trying to set a speed record for lost phones."

A man came in and ordered a coffee in a takeaway cup. Emma noticed him because it was unusual to see someone in jeans at this time of day. So ubiquitous were the fun-seeking colourful skiers, that it was the plainly dressed locals who stood out. He spotted Leon and approached their table.

"Ah, Mr Muller. How are you? Have you got the paperwork for me?" he said, with a smile that fell almost immediately.

Leon shook his head and picked at his pancake. The man audibly exhaled through his nose.

"You are leaving it down to the wire, Mr Muller. I have investors. When?"

"I am thinking about it," Leon said.

The man shook his head. He looked at Emma.

Leon's chair screeched as he pushed it back. He stood up, nose to nose with the guy.

"We are having our breakfast. I said I'd get back to you before the deadline. I will."

The man looked at his watch and sighed. He nodded, to Leon and then to Emma, and left the cafe.

"What was that about?" Emma asked.

"Let's ski," Leon replied.

She pulled her hair into a ponytail and unfurled her wool hat. As she put some bank notes into the dish, she noticed a quarter of a pancake left on Leon's plate. It nearly made her gasp.

"We'll go fast today," he said. "Speed is our friend."

He held the door open for Emma, who stepped out into the town square.

"Leon, who was that guy?"

They walked across the square to the rental shop, to pick up their skis and boots.

"You know I mentioned Sophie got sick?" he said. "Well, it was expensive. And we spent all we had. Whatever it takes. But the repayments are heavy and I can't keep up without selling the cabin to clear the debt."

Emma gasped. "No!"

Leon kicked through fresh, powdery snow. He looked at her, his eyes sloping sadly.

"Yes, it breaks my heart. But look, it's just money. It'll be okay in the end. You're here for two more days, and I don't want to waste them feeling sad. So let's just not think about it, okay?"

She squeezed his hand, and he gave a smile. When they reached his shop, Emma went inside and collected their stuff while Leon sat on the bench in front.

After Emma's first run, the fire was back in Leon's eyes. The sky was clear, and the slope ahead was blue corduroy, sparkling in the morning sun. Leon, his skis jammed in the snow at the side of the slope, crouched in front of Emma and put his arms around her thighs.

"Leon, we're in public," she joked.

With a firm hand on her legs and his head by her hips, he pulled her toward the tips of her skis. She jabbed her poles into the snow to stop herself from tumbling forward.

"Emma, let go of the poles. I want you to lean against the fronts of your boots until the backs of your skis lift from the ground."

She gingerly shifted her weight forward and felt her shins push against the padding inside her ski boots.

"More," he said. His strong arms gripped just below her bum, and she wasn't sure if he was trying to make her cartwheel head-over-heels or if he was there to prevent it from happening. She leaned even further forward, her stomach and lower back straining at the effort of holding her body at a Michael Jackson lean angle. The plastic tongue of her boot dug into her shin and her core shook. She looked back and saw a tiny shadow where the backs of her skis had lifted an inch from the snow.

Leon scurried behind her, with his shoulders behind her thighs and his head to the side of her hips.

"Now back. Lean so far back that the tips of your skis come up."

This took much less effort on Emma's part, and with straining quads she watched the tips of her skis hover an inch above the snow. Leon resurfaced and explained the point of his lesson.

"Emma, you are naturally sitting back, all the time. And that's why you can't turn quickly. You pick up too much speed, and then you sit back even more. You need to get your weight centred over your ski, which will feel like leaning forward."

"Why do I want the backs of my skis to lift up?" she said.

"You don't. I just wanted you to know that even when you think you're going to go over the handlebars, you never will. Think about how hard you had to lean to even get the tails to lift *this* much? Do you want to practise again, to get the feeling of really leaning into your ski tips?"

"No thanks, Leon. We'll get arrested."

They set off down the slope, and he shouted at her to lift the backs of her skis. Sure enough, when she shifted her weight forward, her turns initiated quicker and she was able to sweep across the mountain in satisfying arcs. They skied all the way down to an arcane, two-person lift that crawled slowly and noisily. It didn't even have a safety bar, and Emma wriggled to the very back of the seat. Below them, skiers and snowboarders carved great S-turns down the groomed run. To their left, a forest of dark fir trees was packed in like sharpened pencils.

"Leon, notice that other ski instructors aren't wrapped around their students' waists," she said.

"Emma, notice that other students aren't doing parallel turns on blue runs on their third day."

"Day four," she said, with a slight sadness to her voice.

"I don't think yesterday counts. We only went uphill."

At the top of the slope, the view was awesome in the truest sense of the word. Beyond a wooden piste map surrounded by skiers was a vast, treeless bowl, like a God-sized baseball mitt. The mountaintops looked like torn strips of paper stacked into the distance until they blurred with the sky. Emma stared into the hazy distance, mesmerised by its scale.

"Austria," Leon said.

"Huh?"

He put an arm around her shoulder and raised his ski pole like a telescope.

"The sun rises over Austria, and little Liechtenstein. To the north is Germany, then the sun sets over France, and to our south is Italy. We're actually nearest to Italy from here. Let's go! Your goal is 25 kilometres per hour."

She pulled her goggles down and checked her pockets were zipped, terrified of losing her phone again.

"I don't use kilometres," she said. "I'm British."

"Fine. Your goal is 25 miles per hour."

"That's now how it works, Leon," she called ahead as he skated into a busy blue run. Emma leaned into the fronts of her boots and whooshed after him, swallowing her nerves in desperation to hit the new goal.

The restaurant at the summit of the mountain was elbow to elbow with skiers ferrying trays to their tables, and Emma had to squeeze in to take her seat opposite him. She hovered a hand over her tartiflette.

"Our food only just came," he said, making a start on his fries. "Despite how it looks."

Leon wore a white cable knit sweater with a Swiss flag proudly stitched into the front. The sumptuous collar stood up around his neck like a scarf, nestling against his deeply tanned jawline.

"Emma, you are my sugar mama," he said, licking barbeque sauce from his fingertips.

"It's only a burger, Leon. Well, was. And considering you won't let me pay you for ski lessons anymore, or chip in for my room and board, I'm still considerably in your debt."

Emma smiled and tucked in. Her phone screen flashed with incoming messages and she flipped it to face down, grimacing slightly.

"Work crisis?" he asked.

She nodded, sadly.

"The new Swiss client?"

"I'm impressed, Leon."

"What's their problem? Tell me about your job."

"Careful what you wish for," she sighed. Emma leaned in and spoke quietly, to avoid anyone overhearing.

"I work for a London law firm that specialises in communications. Specifically, making sure any messaging holds up to scrutiny in case of lawsuits. We normally get hired when a company is about to go to court, and wants to control their image as best they can. Damage control. This new client is a big international corporation, tens of thousands of staff. They make drugs."

"The mafia?" he said.

"Good one. But herein lies the problem. They made a drug that got used recreationally a little too often. That happens all the time, but this company is being accused of doing nothing about it. Turning a blind eye, as it were."

"What drug?" he asked.

"Axatil. It's for ADHD," she whispered.

"I have heard of that. It's a big problem in Zurich. One of my old school friends had problems with it."

"That's awful. Did he have ADHD?"

"I don't think so. Me and Sophie hung out with a bad crowd in Zurich, which is why we came up here after college. Off the radar. Off the grid. We wanted the quiet life."

Emma nodded, finishing up her side salad.

"Are you going to get a new job?" he asked.

"Why?"

"I don't know. I got the sense your work is a bit intense," he said.

"I just need to work my way up. This is just life for people in their first few years out of law school. They work you to the bone and if you don't keep up, they replace you with the next newcomer, fresh out of law school and eager to please. It's cutthroat."

"Okay," he said. "It's basically the same thing for ski instructors."

"Really?"

He tucked his chair in to let a fellow instructor pass. The lady, grey haired and deeply tanned, nodded to Leon. "Any eggs?" she asked. He shook his head, and looked back at Emma.

"Not really. I just wanted to empathise. But it's good that the senior people aren't so stressed. That there's a light at the end of the tunnel."

She thought of her boss, Nigel, who had survived two heart attacks before his fiftieth birthday. A man whose angry emails destroyed keyboards and careers, and who burned through assistants on a monthly basis.

She swallowed, and pushed the remainder of her dinner away from her. Leon hoovered it up.

The plateau at the summit was awash with colour, as groups of tourists planned their afternoon. Instructors gathered their pupils and led them down the mountain like mother ducks. Leon extracted his skis from a rack, which had become buried by the lunchtime rush.

"Emma, are you sure you don't mind?" he said.

"Honestly, my legs are shot. You go and do the lesson; I've got some things to take care of in town. I need to call my assistant and see if he's still my assistant."

Emma wiggled the plastic toe of her boot into the C-shaped binding, then stamped the heel into place.

"Are you still looking for a hotel?" Leon asked.

"I should," she said, unconvincingly.

"I planned dinner already," he said.

"You're the best. Well okay. Thank you,"

Emma pushed forcefully on her poles to get moving. She began to pick up some momentum and cruised away from Leon, down a gently sloping green run that led to the village.

"Lean forward!" he shouted.

Emma spent the afternoon in the gorgeous town. At first, she wondered how anyone survived in a town that seemed to only sell snow globes, fridge magnets and dream catchers. But as she explored the side streets, she found hidden shops, where locals could find a box of nails or a cake tin. In a quirky bookstore with shelves stacked to the ceiling, she found a selection of Charles Dickens novels, but didn't know which ones Leon was missing.

Later she discovered a hunting shop, and open-mindedly admired the craftsmanship of the curved rifle stocks in dark walnut. She snapped a picture of a curly-horned sheep head mounted to the wall and pinged it to her dad with the caption '*They hunt sheep!*'

Alongside the red Swiss Army knives beneath the glass counter, she spotted a digital camera with straps to affix it to a tree. The box had a monotone picture of a marmot and the claims that the battery lasted three months. *Perfect for a nature lover*, she thought, adding it to her newly acquired backpack.

Emma sat outside a cafe in the town square and checked her phone for messages from Leon. Finding none, she resorted to browsing her calendar. Her flight home was in just two days, and her feelings about it were mixed. She dreaded having to see Kendal at the airport, no doubt showing off his tan and dragging a new pair of skis through the airport like a Victorian hunter returning from safari. Worse, she would have to sit with him for two hours on the flight.

She flicked to an app which controlled the heating at her flat, showing a lowly twelve degrees. Sure, it would heat up soon enough on her return, but she couldn't shake the image of having to return to a cold, lonely bed. On the plus side, she could barely imagine the joy of opening a drawer full of clean underwear, and not having to rifle through a bag or check a heated towel rail.

Emma's calendar for the following week was stacked with colourful rectangles, each representing a meeting or call. She had to schedule in fifteen minutes to grab a sandwich, or lunch would be squeezed out of existence. There was no time to think, no time to breathe. Only ten-minute slithers in which she could resurface between meetings, gasp for air, and then dive back into a new set of clauses and deal points.

Still, she was glad to be relevant and needed. She had to work her way up a ladder, and hoped one day she could upgrade from a flat to a little mews house with a garden. Her mum would have been so proud to see her farm girl in a sharp suit.

Emma tapped a message to Leon, asking him if he wanted to meet her at the cafe. She pulled her hat over her ears and slid her phone slightly beyond reach, eager to escape the nagging pull of her work.

Chapter Twenty

♥

"How was your new client?" Emma asked, as they walked through the forest trail to Leon's cabin.

"He was pretty funny. Older guy, white hair and gruff. Wheezy. The type of guy who climbs Mount Everest, but with fifty sherpas carrying his stuff. Anyway, he wanted 'extreme'. We skied some runs through the trees, but that wasn't enough, and he wanted something to tell the grandkids. So, I took him up to that bowl we looked at this morning, and we hiked a ridgeline to a tight gully, so narrow you can't turn. Straight shot. Kind of like my dream lesson we talked about."

"Yikes. Did he do it?" Emma asked.

"I asked if he was sure he was up to it, and he breezed it off like it was no big deal. He dropped in and immediately shit himself and turned, which is the worst thing you can do. His skis hit the rocks and they popped right off. He sort of snowballed down, perhaps 500 feet of slope and out onto a powder field. I collected his stuff and skied down to him."

"Was he hurt?"

"No, he was fine. Dazed, spitting snow out of his mouth and scooping it out of his goggles. I said *that's something to tell the grandkids*, and he laughed. After that he asked if I knew any good blue runs."

They laughed as they kicked off their boots and entered the cabin. Without needing to be asked, Emma set to work lighting the stoves, and Leon checked on the chickens. She went out to help and found an egg among the straw.

"That's dinner sorted," she said.

Leon examined a bent piece of chicken wire near the roofline.

"I think a fox or a marten has had a go at this," he said.

He wrestled the wire flat against the wood and went to fetch a hammer. Emma remained in the chicken coop, which was cold but cosy, with a couple of lights giving it a straw-coloured glow. She crouched and offered her hand to an inquisitive hen, who stepped forward on a shelf. Emma scooped her up and gently stroked the soft white feathers, dappled with dark grey spots. The bird looked something like a dalmatian puppy in her arms, and Leon laughed when he saw them together.

"Little Nell loves to cuddle," he said.

"Not surprised. It's pretty cold in here. Do they have no heating all winter?"

"No, they are hardcore," Leon said, ever the proud father.

"But it must get so cold at night."

"They are Swiss chickens. Appenzellers. They are bred to be fine right down to minus ten or fifteen."

Emma gently stroked Little Nell's neck with her index finger, rocking maternally.

"You know what a wattle and comb is?" Leon asked.

Emma nodded.

"Seriously?" he said.

She laughed.

"I grew up on a farm," she said. "This bit."

Emma touched the fleshy pink protrusion that ran like a mohawk from the base of the beak to the top of Nell's head.

"If it gets properly cold, like minus twenty, I have to put grease on those parts to stop frostbite," Leon explained.

Emma set the bird back in a nest of straw.

"Everyone needs a bit of grease on their wattle when it gets cold," she said.

He chuckled.

"I like it in here," Emma said. "It reminds me of home. Home, home. Not London."

"They are really cool animals," he said. "In Summer, they wander round all over the place. They chase Jasmine, it makes me smile. What was the farm like that you were brought up on?"

"There were tough times," Emma said. "But the farm itself was magical. Lambs in the spring. Cats everywhere. It was a really special place to be a kid. Hey, speaking of animals, I have something for you."

Emma rushed to the house to retrieve the wildlife camera and handed it to Leon.

"Whoa. For me? That's so cool!" he said, reading the box.

They set it up in the front yard of the house, overlooking the chicken coup.

"You can make it send you a notification when it is triggered by movement," Emma said.

Leon pulled out his ancient phone and Emma laughed.

"It's compatible with smartphones, not bricks. But we can connect it to mine."

She linked the devices up and devised a test, waiting on the swing by the fire pit while Leon pounced in front of the chicken coup like a bear. Her cackle confirmed it was working. Leon joined her in an Adirondack chair, where he lazily fried burgers on a barbecue that looked like it had never been cleaned. Emma asked for hers to be well done.

"So, does this mean you are going to spy on me from London?" he asked.

"For the sake of your privacy, I'll unlink it," she said.

"I don't mind. I think you'll be disappointed how much action you see, apart from me leaving and arriving back each day. Also, I don't know how much longer I have, here," he said.

"Oh really? I can't imagine you living anywhere else," Emma said. "How come?"

"I have to sell this place. I don't want to. It's a long story." Leon sighed. "I might go to Zurich. Maybe I could come to London, one day," he suggested, lifting the mood a little.

"Would you like to?" she asked.

"Of course. I could see the places from Charles Dickens books. He had a house in Camden," he said, pronouncing it as if it were a den of cams.

Leon took a brioche bun from a paper bag and slid a burger into it.

"There is a bag of salad in the kitchen," he said.

"It's okay," she said. "I'm hardcore."

No sooner had Leon perked up than Emma felt glum.

"I'm not looking forward to going back," she said.

She bit into her burger and gave Leon a thumbs up.

"Because of Kendal?"

"No. I miss Kendal like a hole in the head. Although we did share a lot of friends, so that will be difficult. Did I tell you what Bella said? *Boys will be boys*, basically. And she was my favourite of his friends. No, it's just London. I've got the dread."

"If you are bored of London, you are bored of life," said Leon. "Isn't that the saying?"

"Yes. And I am indeed bored of both London and life, so the saying is probably right. It's not London's fault, of course. It has the best theatres, shops, restaurants, everything. But I don't do any of that, so what does it matter? When I first got to London, I planned to see Swan Lake. The ballet."

"I know what Swan Lake is," he said.

"Sorry, it's just sometimes you know things, like Tchaikovsky and Dickens, but yesterday you didn't know what an app was."

"What is it again?" he asked.

"An application. Oh, stop messing with me!" Emma said.

He smiled. "So, what's the end of your sob story? Poor Emma never got to see Swan Lake?"

"Maybe," she said coyly.

"That is the most first world problem I've ever heard," he said. "Let me find my tiny violin."

Emma snatched the burger from Leon's hand and took a massive bite. She stared him in the eye, her face reddening as she attempted to chew it and suppress her laughter. He grabbed what was left, examining the remaining crescent with sad eyes.

"That was a low blow," he said.

Emma finally swallowed and made a kiss motion with her fingers.

"You have stolen most of my meals so far, Leon. Shall we go inside?" she said. "I should get the fires going. It'll be getting dark soon."

"I'll catch you up. I have some things to sort out outside."

Leon entered the front door with his coat hanging open and a schoolboy grin on his face. He was flushed from activity and wiped the sweat from his brow. Emma sat at the dining table, where she tried to read a forty-page contract on her tiny phone screen.

"You're looking a bit pleased with yourself," she said. "Someone been greasing their wattle?"

He whisked past her to a door which she had thus far remained unopened, next to the bathroom. A few minutes later he emerged with two pairs of white ice skates, slung over his shoulder by their long black laces. Their metal blades clattered as he approached her.

"Have you got another rental shop in there?" she asked.

"Just a storage cupboard," he said. "It's a mess."

He carefully extracted the phone from her fingers and set it down on the table. He led her by the hand toward the front door, his smile infecting her with excitement.

"Do I need my coat?" she said.

"It's winter in Switzerland. You always need your coat."

In front of Leon's cabin was a yard with a massive tree stump in its centre, bearing the wounds and dents of Leon's log-splitting axe. Emma passed a pickup truck so thick with snow that she could only guess what colour it was, and followed Leon around the side of the chicken house.

"Ta da," he said.

She looked out over a frozen pond about the size of a tennis court. Around its edge was a hip-high bank of snow with a shovel jammed in it victoriously. The sky was a mellow wash of yellow and peach, with wisps of cloud slashed across here and there.

Emma pulled Leon close, feeling the warmth pour off his neck.

"I love ice skating," she said, lifting the smaller pair of skates off his shoulders. Emma looked at the label inside the leather tongue and shrugged. The size was close enough, and she perched on the chicken coop step and pulled them on.

Leon emerged with Madame Defarge bundled up at his chest. He staggered down to the pond, where the bird spilled out onto the ice.

"Oh, they're joining us?" Emma said.

She heard Leon clap loudly inside the coop and a dozen chickens came pouring out onto the icy path. Emma lifted her legs up to clear the way for them to reach their leader, who was eagerly exploring the pond. The chickens dispersed across the frozen expanse, slipping, and flapping in confusion and excitement.

Leon pulled his skates on and together they stepped down the path and joined the birds on the pond.

"Do you need me to hold you?" he said, watching carefully as she stepped out onto the ice.

"No, I'll be okay. Just give me a minute before I start doing pirouettes."

Leon skated off, head forward and shoulders down like a hockey player. He swept around the ice in a circuit, stepping his feet over each other as he cornered. The chickens pecked around, seemingly unconcerned by the missile that dodged between them. Emma plucked the shovel out of the snowbank for support, pushing herself along like a gondolier. She hadn't ice skated since the birthday parties of her primary school years, but she had rollerbladed at university and the motion felt familiar. Emma quickly advanced from walking clumsily across the ice to gliding along for a few feet at a time. Leon swooped in and put his arms out to hold her.

"No way," she said. "I know what you're like when you get into instructor mode. You'll throw my skate into a bush."

The chickens took short, messy flights and perched on the snowbank before returning to the ice. Emma's confidence built with each lap of the pond, until she was wobbling alongside Leon. They linked hands, and skated around and around, taking in the view of the forest, the yard and the house, with its column of smoke rising into the dusky sky.

"Does your phone have music in it?" Leon asked.

"Of course. I get reception out here, so *in it* you will find every song in the world. What do you want to listen to?"

"Swan Lake, obviously," he said.

She stopped skating, and Leon continued to loop around. She watched a chicken take a brief flight out of Leon's path, and then collapse on her belly on landing, sliding across the ice.

"Ah, these are our swans?" she said. "You are adorable."

For a moment she was overwhelmed by emotion for this man she had originally miscast as a brutish oaf. She thumbed through Spotify and selected Swan Lake. She held out two white earbuds, and they took one each.

"Which track?" she asked, bewildered by the selection.

Leon skated around her in a tight ellipse, like a planet circling its sun.

"We start at the beginning, of course. Act one," he said.

"Okay. I like your commitment. What happens in act one?"

"You don't know Swan Lake?" he said.

"You don't know Spotify!" she retorted. "I never got to see it. Remember? Teach me!"

He skidded to a stop in front of her and tucked her hair aside so he could see her face.

"You are so beautiful," he said, taking her hands in his and skating backward. She looked into his blue eyes and wanted to pull him into her for a kiss, but his momentum was too strong.

"Is this part of the story?" she said.

"No," he said, dropping her hands and skidding to a stop. "We start now."

"I am a carefree, spoiled rich guy,"

"Kendal," she said.

"And you are my mother," he said.

"Sexy."

"You are annoyed at me for always partying. You say I have to find a bride at the ball. Go!"

Leon skated off, doing spins and weaving in and out of chickens. Emma did her best to catch up.

"Hey son," she said. "All this skating and spinning. It's getting you nowhere."

"Mom, leave me be. I love to skate and spin," he said.

"No, you need a bride. Get a suit. You're going to the ball," Emma said.

Leon screeched to a dramatic stop, spitting ice up.

"Ugh," he said, like a moody teenager. "Next track."

It took Emma a moment to realise these last couple of words were stage direction. She took out her phone and skipped to act two. She recognised immediately the dulcet sound of a violin, delicate and foreboding. This was classic Swan Lake.

"I'm hunting swans," he said.

"Who hunts swans?"

"I do. But I'm just about to shoot one when it turns into a beautiful princess."

Emma took her cue and skated off to the far side of the pond. She gingerly approached a chicken who had become tired of playing and rested on the ice. Emma scooped her up and hid behind the bundle of mottled white feathers.

"That beautiful swan. I will shoot it!" Leon shouted. He put the blade of the snow shovel into his shoulder and aimed the wooden handle at Emma and Little Nell.

As the music built dramatically in their ears, she returned the chicken onto the ice and rose. She put one leg behind the other, and angled her back foot so only the tip of her skate blade touched the ice. Despite wearing a ski jacket, she did her best to be an elegant princess, connecting her fingertips above her head to make a delicate egg shape with her arms.

Leon tossed the shovel over his shoulder and skated towards her, dropping to his knees and sliding in like a rock star. Emma looked askance, surprising herself with her ability to keep a straight face as she stared into the deep pink sky.

"Don't worry," he said dramatically. "I won't hurt you, princess. What did you say? That you are a human by night and a swan by day? You were cursed by the owl? Then I'll kill the owl!"

"Yes," Emma said. "You must!"

"No," Leon exclaimed.

"That's what I meant. Don't do it!" Emma said.

"Only true love can break the curse. Act three," Leon said. "We're at a ball now. You are a girl *pretending* to be Odette, trying to seduce me. One second. If I don't put them in now, they'll fly up to the trees to roost."

He picked up Madame Defarge and delivered her to the hen coop. Emma skated around, clapping at the other chickens and herding them toward their home. After a few minutes, the chickens were back inside, and Leon slid the bolt shut. The sky was getting dark, and he waved at the house to make a flood light come on.

"Where were we?" he asked, slipping gracefully back onto the ice.

"The ball," she said, skipping to the next track. It began with epic trumpets and cymbals that conjured images of a hilltop castle. Leon began to dance across the ice, angling his feet out to the sides and spinning in a circle. Emma skated around him, doing her best to show off by skating on one leg with her other sticking out behind her.

"Wow! Odette, you are truly magical. We must marry," he said, pulling Emma into him. For a moment she felt the warmth of Leon's lips brush against hers. He suddenly pulled away, and Emma opened her eyes and regained her balance.

"Wait, you are not the real Odette! I must go back to the lake and find her," he said.

He skated off, shouting "The fourth and final act. You are now stuck as a swan forever."

"Can I talk?" she said.

"Yes, but you would rather die than be a swan for the rest of your life."

With Leon at the edge of the pond, Emma crouched in the middle, her arm above her head and fingertips touching like a bird beak. An epic violin concerto played in their ears as Leon skated toward her.

"Odette! I am so sorry I was tricked. You are my true love. But it is too late."

"I would rather DIE than be a swan, forever," Emma said, collapsing theatrically onto the ice in a heap.

"Then I will die with you," Leon said, nuzzling behind her in the middle of the pond, big spoon, little spoon. Emma pulled his hand over her hip, and he reached up to her chest and pulled her into him. The warmth of his body engulfed her.

"Is this the end," she whispered.

"Yes," Leon said. She turned to face him, and their eyes connected. She reached up to his face and brushed the hair from his cheek with her thumb, pushing it back behind his ear. His skin was dark in the pale moonlight, but his eyes seemed to glow.

"You are so beautiful, Emma," he said, his fingertip brushing against the dimple as she smiled. They both inched toward each other, their lips meeting. On a bed of ice, under a blanket of an inky, star-studded sky, their tongues connected. Nervously, at first, but then dancing in the darkness. Passionately writhing, unleashing a desire that she hadn't realised had built into a fire. Her eyes tight shut, the feeling of time and place disappeared. There was only her and Leon, and in that moment she felt wanted - loved even - in a way she barely knew existed. For what might have been minutes or hours, they kissed on the frozen lake, neither wanting the moment to end.

They drifted onto their backs and stared up into the night. Hand in hand, they kicked lazily at the ice with the heels of their skates, digging tiny holes with the spurs of the blades.

Their breaths became synchronised, forming columns of mist that swam toward the moon and disappeared.

"Do you feel like an actor still on stage after the curtain is closed?" Leon asked.

"I feel like a member of the audience so knocked out by the performance she just witnessed, that she's still in her seat, hours after they've locked the theatre shut."

"Our Swan Lake was pretty good," Leon said, leaning on his elbow.

"Five stars. A triumph," she said.

"But we might go the way of the main characters if we stay out here any longer."

He climbed to his feet and pulled her up.

Once inside Emma hung her coat on the peg and handed Leon her skates. She watched him carry them to the cupboard door, but he hung them over the handle rather than enter it. She put the backs of her hands onto her cheeks.

"Are you cold?" he said, feeding a log onto the stove.

"I can't tell," she replied. "This house feels like an oven. So I'm probably frozen, like one of your fish fingers."

He rubbed his hands together rapidly then touched her neck, his fingers caressing the soft skin where her jaw met her ears. She closed her eyes and met his lips once again. Without saying a word, Leon led her into his bedroom. Jasmine jumped off the couch and followed, but he toed the door shut.

Chapter Twenty-One

E mma stood on the frozen pond with her hat pulled so tight that the bobble bruised her scalp. Her jaw nestled into the soft fabric of her jacket collar, and each outgoing breath gave her cheeks a blast of warmth, but then left them slightly damp and icy as she inhaled. The sun glowed over the distant peaks, but thoughts the previous day's hike were long gone.

"I don't know where your head is at, frankly," said her boss, Nigel.

"The reception here is bad," Emma said. "I wasn't ignoring you; I can assure you."

He grunted. "It's not good enough. When I was in your position, I wouldn't have swanned off for a week during an important client approach."

She thought, briefly, of the swans. Chickens involuntarily dancing on slippery ice, as she and Leon listened to an orchestra through one ear.

"Are you there? For god's sake," he said.

A series of bangs came through the earpiece, loud enough that she had to move the phone away from her head.

"I'm here," she said, closing her eyes to focus. "I have looked for flights, non-stop, but it's the school holidays and they're booked solid."

"Can't you work there?" he barked. "You have your laptop, I assume."

There was a frosty silence.

"It's Friday, and.." she began, deflecting the question.

"I know what day it is," he said.

"...and I fly back on Monday evening. I'll be back in the office on Tuesday first thing."

"That's nearly a week away!" he said.

Inside her left mitten, Emma began to count on her fingers.

"I will review the new documents today," she said.

"I should hope so. We need to show them we don't mess around. I gave it to the others, but their work was a pile of crap. I expect a reply in my inbox by close of business. Emma, I had you earmarked for taking the lead on this client, and you know that's a big pay jump. But honestly, I'm having second thoughts."

"It will be there," she said. "Hello?"

The line was dead.

Emma returned to the house and crept inside. It was only just seven, which meant her boss's tirade had begun at six in the UK. She shuddered to think what life must be like for his family. She sat at the dining table and searched for flights to London. She found one via Barcelona, which would take all day to get home and cost an eye-watering amount. Nonetheless, her thumb tapped the button to book it, but reception was lost and a blank webpage emerged. She slapped the phone down on the table.

Leon emerged from the bedroom in his boxer shorts. He had the body of an athlete, wide muscular thighs and calves so defined that it looked like simply standing on tiptoes would launch him off the ground. His stomach was a neat mogul field of bumps, two rows slightly misaligned. His arms crossed his torso, and he gripped his own shoulders with his strong hands.

"It's cold," he said, adding a lovable 'brrr'.

Emma, still in her ski jacket and hat, smiled politely but did not allow his body to distract her. She focused on her phone, pinching and zooming to examine lines of small print in a contract. Leon crouched by the unlit stove, making a nest of straw firelighters and laying on a handful of kindling. Emma peered over the top of her device at his long, smooth back and his bum. She switched chairs to face away from him.

"You're up early," he said. "Did I snore?"

"No," she said. "I got a call from work which woke me. My boss wanted to urgently tell me how useless I am."

"Did you tell him about the week you have had?" Leon asked. She shook her head.

"No, Leon. He's not interested in my relationship drama. He doesn't want to hear that this whole trip was Kendal's stupid surprise, and that the idiot forgot my laptop, and that I'm stuck in a cabin with no signal. He's got all the warmth of a shark," she snapped, with all the warmth of a shark.

Jasmine sat politely by Emma's feet, pulling back as if to prepare for a jump. Emma slid her chair forward so her legs were under the table. Leon raised his eyebrows.

"I'm going in the shower," he said, disappearing for some time.

Emma rooted around the kitchen for something on which to write notes. She ransacked the kitchen until she found the miscellaneous drawer which every home has. A lighter, elastic band, a couple of AA batteries of dubious charge, a twist tie, and a pen. On the kitchen worktop she found a stack of papers held down by a chicken-shaped egg basket. She flicked through some serious looking bills with a Swiss flag on the header, stamped with the word overdue. Determined not to let her curiosity get the better of her, she stuffed one into its envelope, onto which she could scribble notes.

At the dining table, she continued her work, writing in cramped lettering to make the most of her tiny notepad. Emma was desperate to find some redeeming behaviour on the part of the pharmaceutical giant, but no amount of pinching and zooming could reveal any. By her literal back-of-the-envelope calculations, for every million dollars in profit, the corporation had spent five dollars on rehab centres, plus a further fifty dollars crowing about it. It was extremely hard to find an angle from which their potential client didn't appear to be a soulless money hoover.

Leon emerged from the shower wrapped in a towel. Emma closed her eyes.

"Are you okay?" he said.

She waved him along.

"Finally got some signal," Emma said, brushing her boots on the doormat and flicking back her hood.

"Are you finished with work?" Leon asked, hopefully. "Shall we hit the slopes?"

"No, I had to download more documents," Emma said. "I'll see how I feel after lunch."

"I have a lesson this afternoon. Extreme Man wants more danger," Leon shrugged.

Emma crouched by a socket on the wall and inserted her charger. The cable strung taut between the outlet and the table. She tried awkwardly to hold it to the table, whilst tapping on the screen. She tapped a message to her mum, which read *'9am and already sent a fifteen-page email. #lawyerlife'*

She didn't know why she included the hashtag. Her mum had passed away long before the advent of Twitter. But none of it made any sense and it wasn't the day to linger on thoughts of the afterlife.

"Who are you texting?" he asked.

Emma sighed. "Nobody."

He nodded.

"Leon, I've got to get back to my job. I'm really worried I'm going to get fired."

She stared at the wooden grain of the table, her forehead resting on her palms. A headache formed behind her eyes.

"Emma, do you like being a lawyer?" he asked.

He offered a smile which was not reciprocated.

"I trained for seven years. I love my job."

Her answer had a mechanical rhythm to it, like the words were only meant to shoot down thoughts of dissent.

"What do you like about it?" he pressed.

Emma shot him a defensive look.

"I like everything about it. I just can't do it when I'm up a mountain. I need to be back in London."

"Right," he said, cautiously. "It's just that when I see you think about work, you..."

She raised her eyebrows.

"Become Mean Emma?"

"No, no. Sorry, I'll make coffee."

The percolator bubbled and Leon poured out two coffees.

"My mum," she confessed, realising the irony of her keeping secrets, after the television debacle. "I was texting my mum. You must think I'm completely mad."

He placed her drink in front of her, but she remained in her own world, staring down at the surface of the table. .

"Not a bit," he said, his hand on her shoulder blade. "I talk to Sophie when I visit the cemetery. Is it any different?"

"I suppose not," Emma sighed.

"If you don't mind me asking, what happened to your mum?"

Emma closed her eyes and a pause lingered in the air.

"Don't worry," Leon said. "Forget I asked."

He sat next to her and tried to make sense of the calculations she had scrawled on the envelope.

"I was never late for school," she began, her voice soft and starting to crack. "My brother Marley was, but not me. I packed my back as soon as I got home and put it by the door for the next day. But for whatever reason, I was running late. And once we missed that bus, that was it. There was only one bus each way. So Mum gave me a lift. Roads were icy and the gritter trucks hadn't been out. As she dropped me off she said 'Go get 'em, tiger', which sticks in my mind because she never said things like that."

The cabin was silent, but for the sound of Emma's forceful, controlled breaths. In through the nose, out through the mouth.

"I'm so sorry," Leon said.

Emma made a noise so faint, yet so laden with the pain of regret.

"It's not your fault, Emma," he said.

"That's what I tell myself," she replied, swallowing down the emotion. "But it's hard, even after all these years."

"I bet it is. But your mum wouldn't have blamed you, and you can't blame yourself. Kids miss the school bus in every town, in every country. None of what happened that day is your fault. You were just a kid who missed the bus. You were just a kid."

He rubbed on her shoulder, as if to wake her from the dark nightmare. She stood up, catching the charging cable that strung between the table and the outlet. Her phone was dragged off the edge, banging as it hit the wooden floor.

"Damn it!" she said, thumbing a crack on the glass screen.

"This isn't going to work," she scowled.

"It's broken?"

"Not my stupid phone. This!" Emma motioned around to the interior of the cabin. She crouched by the charging cable and yanked it from the wall. With an almost violent fervour, she wrapped the cable around the plug and slam-dunked it into her backpack.

"Emma, we can move the table. Shall I see if anyone has a laptop you can borrow?"

Leon began to shift the dining table toward the wall, but it was too late.

She went to the bathroom and wrenched her underwear from the towel rail, stuffing it into the bag.

"Leon, you've been so kind. Really. You are the best. But I've got to go. You've got your life here, I've got my life there. This. It was...something."

"Something?"

Leon crossed his arms.

"What do you want? I literally just came out of a long relationship. I don't know what I'm doing. My life is unravelling."

She bustled into the bedroom and scooped up her few items of makeup and face cream, dumping them into the bag.

"But there are no hotels in town," Leon said.

"There are. One called me yesterday and I didn't tell you because I wanted to stay."

Leon followed her into the bedroom as she furiously packed.

"So stay!" he said. "I love having you here. Please, Emma. Let's just talk this through."

Emma crouched over the bag and pulled the drawstring shut. She blew the hair up and out of her face, and looked up at Leon.

"I've got a career, Leon. I worked for it for a decade, and it's about to go down the toilet because I'm here fucking around in Switzerland with sledges and skis and wine. I'm not about to lose everything. I'm sorry."

He snorted angrily.

"I didn't ask you to lose everything. I get it, your career is important. I can see that. But don't pretend this was just fun. We have something, Emma. Me and you."

Emma approached him, took the percolator from his fingers and placed it on the counter. She looked into his eyes and raised her hands, taking his fingers into hers. She exhaled, slowly.

"Leon, you are wonderful. You really are. You took me in and I am so grateful. You have to understand though, I am rebounding off a long relationship, and I'm not making good decisions."

He squeezed her hands tight and looked at her backpack.

"*This* is a bad decision, Emma. Don't you see? Your job makes you miserable."

Emma released his grip and pushed his hands away. She marched over to the hatstand and pulled her coat from it, knocking Leon's to the floor.

"I have to go. My life is in London. Your life is here. I've only known you for four days, Leon."

"The best four days of my life. Stay with me."

"Here?" she said, looking around as if seeing the cabin for the first time.

"Is that so crazy?"

"Of course it's crazy. I've got a career to fix, five hundred miles away."

"But you don't even like that job."

"Oh my god, you're like Kendal!"

His brow furrowed, head forward like a bull.

"I am *nothing* like Kendal. I don't want you to quit your job so I can make you into someone else. I want you to quit your job because I want the real you. I'm not like Kendal because I would never treat you the way that he did."

He paused for a moment, weighing his words. "I love you, Emma."

She raised her palm to him and looked away, as if to call a halt to this nonsense.

"Four days, Leon. I'm sorry, I'm not going to be a happy housewife for you. This is just a holiday. And now it's time to go back to real life."

He shook his head and leaned back on the fridge, twisting a tea towel in his fists like he might tear it in two. His eyes glazed with anger and frustration and crushing disappointment.

"You have issues, Emma, with your job. And I can help you deal with them. I would do whatever it takes."

She spun to face him, eyes wide and mouth agape.

"I've got issues? Are you kidding me? When you can't even walk into your own ski shop because of..."

She gestured towards the closed bedroom door, behind which lay the shrine to his sister.

Leon stared at her for a moment in silence. Then he swung the tea towel over his shoulder and started dumping crockery into the kitchen sink, yanking the hot tap on.

Emma swung the front door open, the cold air pouring into his warm cabin.

"Leon, I'm sorry. I didn't mean that."

"Whatever," he said.

She hovered in the doorway, backpack knocking against the frame. He stared intently at the bobbing collection of cups and glasses.

"Leon, I didn't want it to end like this."

He fixed his gaze into the dishwater, foam rising into mountains.

"You say, as you literally end it like this. Just go, Emma!"

Steam rose from the sink and fogged the kitchen window. The washing up bowl overflowed as Leon wiped a hole in the condensation to watch Emma trudge into the woods and out of his life.

Chapter Twenty-Two

♥

"Would you like to pay in pounds or Swiss Francs?"

Emma never knew how best to answer this question. Truth is, she only ever pondered this quandary when she was on holiday, and this was definitely not the time to grapple with the machinations of global currency exchange.

"Swiss Francs," she said. Today it was simple enough; she didn't want to know how much this hotel cost, so it was better to pay in Monopoly money. With its 'wellness suite' and staff in sharp green suits, she knew it would not come cheap. She tapped in her pin number and slid the machine back to the smug concierge. Emma had intended to go directly to Zurich and find an early flight to London but then discovered a couple of rooms had become available in town. She couldn't face a train journey with three changes and needed to get her head straight.

Her room was small, but the bed was soft and the view of the pretty town square was irritatingly adorable. It was hard to stay angry at a place with horse drawn sleighs and children building snowmen on every corner. The shower was a savage, needle-blasting assault on her shoulders, and she stood under it until her skin stung and her eyes had run out of tears.

Emma dried her hair on the hotel's hairdryer and sighed at the room's gigantic light switches and overpriced snacks. She sat on her bed, cross-legged, with her freshly charged phone in hand.

Two hours until lunch and no appetite to revisit Leon's shop to take out her skis. It was time to work.

She set about researching the new pharmaceutical client she would be defending. Hitting the ground running was the way to put this awful holiday behind her and assimilate back into London life. She even closed the curtains to make it feel more like her gloomy flat.

The files provided by her law firm read like press releases, with blithe and calculating disregard for the blood on its hands. She dug deeper into court records and newspaper articles, and there were too many people like the one Leon knew in Zurich. The suffering caused to the addicts and the indirect cost to social services was stratospheric, and it was the same story in countless European countries. Lawsuits against the company had stacked up, and now the corporation would face the highest courts in Europe. Emma's role in it would be small, but this could be a career-defining leap which could set her up for life.

Emma tossed her phone onto the bed and peaked out at the world beyond the curtains. In the town square she watched a lady carry a paper bag from the bakery, followed by two young children.

"Dad, it's me," she said.

"I know that. Your name comes up," he said, chipper as anything. "How are the slopes?"

"Well, the slopes are good, but Kendal and I broke up."

"Broke up?"

"Yes. I can't tell you any more about it, because you'll say I told you so and I don't want to cry because I've just done my makeup."

"Okay," he said. "Then all I will say is that you're worth ten of him. Ten thousand. Forget him."

"Thanks," Emma said. "Dad, I was thinking about work."

"Typical," he said.

"I know. That's the problem. Do you think I'm a workaholic?"

Michael thought about this for a moment.

"I don't know, really. You've always worked hard. Workaholic? I'm not sure I know what it means. Am I?"

"Probably. But you're a farmer, so you have to work 80-hour weeks or everything dies. I do the same, but really it's just so that someone, somewhere, makes their bonus."

"People need lawyers," he said. "That's a fact of life."

"But there's two sides to every case, and sometimes I wonder whether I'm with the good guys or the bad guys."

"Have you thought about doing anything else?" he said. "Maybe law isn't for you."

She snorted.

"It's a bit late for a career change now, Dad. It took me seven years to qualify."

He laughed, which took her by surprise.

"Late? You were only just a teenager! You can do whatever you like, Emma. You can always come back to law later in life when you want to. What other things do you enjoy?"

"I don't know. I like being outside. I like people. I don't like arguing."

"Hmm. Lawyering might not be the best idea."

Emma broke her promise to hold it together.

"I just feel like Mum would be disappointed, you know? She wanted so much for me."

"Emma, no. Don't even think that. Your mum *did* want you to go to a great school, and she made sure we had the money to help you get through university. We did that because we wanted you to have options. That's all. Options. Me and her worked the land because that's all we knew. We wanted you and Marley to have choices. I don't know if you noticed, darling, but farming is quite hard."

"I know. And I feel so bad that you did all that for me. For me to then sack it off because the going got tough."

"No, I don't mean it like that. I love farming and don't resent spending that money one jot. I just mean, it's backbreaking work and we wanted to make sure you and Marley weren't lumbered with it, out of destiny. We wanted you to have the qualifications so you could make a choice."

"You don't think she'd be disappointed if I threw it all away? All those years?"

"You're not throwing away a thing. You've still got that qualification if you ever want it. Your mum would be more disappointed if she knew you were stuck on train tracks, doing something you hate. She was adamant that you kids went to a solid school because she wanted you to have a steering wheel. Sounds like it's time to use it."

Emma blew her nose.

"It's just, when I came back, I saw that rocket ship on my old bedroom wall. I remember how hard I had to fight to earn those ticks and blast off into lawyer space. I feel so stupid that I did all that work and now I'm floating around, wishing I had a job in a ski rental shop. Or something like that."

He sighed.

"I am as proud as a peacock, Emma. Your self-discipline is incredible. And I never liked that rocket anyway."

"What's wrong with the rocket?" she asked.

"I don't know. I suppose I felt like you couldn't wait to get a million miles from the farm. And I'd be left on my own, probably on fire from those flappy bits of orange tissue paper."

"Oh, don't be silly," she snorted. "I'll always think of the farm as home. I will think about my career. It's hard to imagine giving up on law so soon. I'm probably just emotional because of the week I've had."

"Well, you're always welcome here, and I'd still be just as proud of you if you worked in a ski rental shop or in a London skyscraper. So would your mum."

"Thanks, dad. Love you."

Would she really be proud, though? Emma pondered, long after the call had ended.

Across the street from the hotel, Emma selected a sandwich from the bakery. She kept looking over her shoulder, since there were now two men she needed to avoid. On her way back to the hotel she passed Leon's rental store, which she gave a wide berth. Despite her efforts, the bell above the door rang and her heart sank when she heard her name. Emma turned around to see Chloe, who was holding the wooden sledge.

"Leon dropped this off. Said you'd probably be by to pick it up," she said.

"Oh. Thanks," Emma said. She glanced up and down the street to check she wouldn't bump into Leon and accepted the sledge. She threaded her arm through a curved runner, and it hung off her shoulder like a backpack.

Chloe hovered for a moment. "Are you okay?"

"Not really," Emma said.

"Leon?" Chloe said, head cocked to the side.

Emma nodded. She forced a smile and raised up her paper bag. "Better get on. It was nice to meet you, Chloe."

"Let's go for a drink when I close up," Chloe said. "I owe you one for rescuing me the other day."

"I can't, I..." Emma began. She thought of her little hotel room, and how her only plans were to brush the snow off a chair on the little balcony and try to eat a sandwich without getting emotional. "Okay, that would be great. Shall we meet in Caspers?"

'Turns out all that glitters isn't gold,' she tapped into a message to her mum.

Emma followed it up with *'Got a bit distracted by my ski instructor.'*

The tirade came thick and fast as Emma unloaded, firing messages into the ether.

'I've been thinking about my career. It's the only reliable thing I have. Going to knuckle down. Should be much easier to focus without men in my life.'

Emma spent the afternoon cramming neat notes onto Hotel Avensis notepaper. Her phone was hot to the touch and she was on her third data bundle. She read through ten years of company reports for her new client, each one a hundred-page document of statements and graphs. Her eyes became dry and twitchy, which she attempted to fix by staring at a distant mountain peak every now and then. It took all of her meditative resolve to shake off images of following Leon up that mountain as night turned to day.

At 4pm she fired off a detailed email to her boss, with a chummy subject line of *'A few more thoughts'*. She bit her fingernails as she waited for a flash of bold lettering that would indicate a reply. Nigel was glued to his phone and replied immediately or never. His inner circle was a clifftop plateau, and his underlings were huddled around him or plummeting to their death. There was no middle ground, and she was desperate to be back on top.

'This is great work, Emma,' came a quick reply.

"Yes!" she said, feeling a rush of endorphins.

Chapter Twenty-Three

E mma rubbed concealer under her eyes, but there was no hiding her lack of sleep last night, early start, and a day of on-off crying. Her phone rang. Normally she would relish a gossipy call from Bella, but she let it ring several more times before drawing a deep breath and answering it.

"Hi Em. I just wanted to check in, really. Make sure you're okay."

Emma wondered what the motive was for this call. A week ago, she would have thought nothing of Bella calling to chit-chat, but Kendal's infidelity had cleaved a rift into the ground, and it was clear which side Bella stood. Over there, champagne flowed freely, grouses got shot, and occasionally the men would satisfy their carnal needs with strangers.

"I'm fine, thanks. I have a room at the Avensis in the square. How was your week?" Emma asked.

"Great. I mean, it was awful what happened with you and Kendal. We are so sad. But the skiing was good."

"I'm glad you had fun," Emma said.

"Speaking of checking in, I have your boarding pass here," Bella said.

"I see. Could you email me the digital version? They can scan it at the gate."

"Actually, he doesn't have that. He can't remember his login and says it's all a faff. Did you want to come by and pick it up?" Bella asked. "I would walk into town, but my legs are jelly."

"Is Kendal there?"

"No. He's out with Charlie."

Emma looked out of the window where streetlights created orbs of light in the diagonal snowfall. It was mesmerising, but her drive to get out there and kick through the snow was gone. Losing Leon had taken away the town's magic, and she knew it was time to gather her things and get out of there. A boarding pass would bring her one step closer to the real world.

"Sure."

The aquamarine hot tub poured steam and chlorine into the night sky. Bella opened the chalet door and the women exchanged a polite embrace that outstayed its welcome. Emma looked down at Bella's bare, manicured feet on the wooden floor, but remained on the mat in her boots.

"Come in!" Bella said, beelining for the wine fridge.

"I won't stay," Emma replied, with a smile.

"The boys won't be back for ages. They're in Caspers."

"Alice?"

"She has the night off. It's her friend's Christening or something," Bella said, pouring prosecco into tall flutes.

Emma couldn't hide her smirk as she processed the improbability of a Christening taking place on this dark night, and a local family inviting a seasonaire. However, she could picture Alice in Caspers right now, and wondered for the first time if Charlie was just as bad as Kendal.

"Are you okay, Em?" Bella asked.

Emma watched the snow build against the floor to ceiling glass, anxious to get back to the hotel before Kendal returned, drunk and obnoxious. Still, she slipped off her shoes and perched on the arm of the sofa.

"So, that sexy ski instructor?" Bella said. "What is the deal with him? Did you stay at his place."

Emma nodded. She accepted the glass from Bella and pinched the delicate stem between her fingertips. Bella pulled her legs up onto the sofa, feigning nonchalance, but Emma began to wonder if this boarding pass nonsense was a ruse to get gossip. She pictured Bella and the boys giggling about what became of Emma and the caveman while they nibbled olives and ate fondue.

"Did you and him, you know...?" Bella asked, puffing a cushion that seemed perfectly puffed.

Emma, still in her coat, gave a short smile, but the time for deep-and-meaningfuls with Bella was over.

"You know, you could have come back. I wish you had. I didn't like the idea of you being out there in the woods, holed up in a creepy cabin."

"It wasn't creepy. But I'm in a hotel now."

"Emma, I'm not going to tell," Bella said, raising her eyebrows. "What did you two get up to?"

"We went skiing, a lot. Did some telemark. Ice skating. Tobogganing." Emma gave her head the slightest shake.

"Sounds actually quite fun," Bella said. "We had a good week too. Apres ski got earlier and earlier, though, until there was no ski at all and the cocktails started in the morning."

"Apres breakfast," Emma said.

Bella laughed. Emma tried to, too, but it was getting harder to stay in that chalet by the minute. Her own failures and naivety were piling up like snow against the windows.

"I should go," Emma said, placing her untouched drink onto the coffee table. "Do you have the ticket?"

Bella picked up a vase from the mantle, under which was a slip of card. She passed it to Emma.

"Look, Emma, once we're back in London, let's still hang out. Okay?"

"Yes," Emma said. "Of course. You have my number. I warn you though, my flat doesn't have a view over the Thames."

"But it has you, Emma."

Emma slid her feet into her boots and tied the laces.

"How does Kendal know about Leon's cabin?" she asked.

"You know Kendal. He has his fingers in a lot of pies," Bella said.

Emma paused mid-bow, the laces hanging limp across her fingers.

"I don't quite know what you mean," she said.

"Remember Kendal was going to invest in a building? He's waiting on Mr Muller – that's your ski instructor – to sign. It was meant to happen this week. Deadline is tomorrow, so he's getting anxious that the deal goes through before we have to leave."

"Kendal's buying a chalet *this week?* He only started talking about it on Monday. He does like to shoot from the hip, doesn't he?" Emma said.

"Well, he's buying the land. It might be ready next year, he thinks. He's been looking at it for a while," Bella said. "And if you see Leon, maybe tell him that time is short. Kendal would love to get this wrapped up before he leaves."

Emma gave a sad smile as she tied up her boots.

"I see. Is that what Kendal asked you to tell me?" Emma said.

Bella sat up from the sofa, hand on chest.

"Not at all, Em. I just raised it because, you know. Forget I said anything."

"I won't have any more ski lessons, but if I see Leon, I'll pass on the message. I have his number, if you want to give it to Kendal?"

"Believe me, the agent has tried and tried," Bella said.

"Right. Well, I hope it works out for them all," Emma said. "I'll see you all on the plane. That won't be awkward."

Emma forced a smile between pursed lips.

"Don't forget to check your toboggan," Bella said.

Emma did a thumbs up and let herself out.

"Thanks for switching to this place," Emma said. "I couldn't risk bumping into my ex. And also, I'm all partied out."

She sat in a booth opposite Chloe and poured a glass of mineral water.

"Caspers is too loud anyway," Chloe said. "This is better. When you want good food in Switzerland, you have to go French or Italian."

"You're not a fan of your country's food?" Emma asked. "That's blasphemy."

"We are at the crossroads of Europe, Emma. We had all the choice in the world. But we chose ... beige."

Emma laughed. "What do you mean?"

"Cheese. Potatoes. Onion. Everything is some yellowy combination of that," Chloe said.

"At least you mastered chocolate," Emma added.

The waiter appeared with a pizza on a wooden board. He set it in the middle of the table along with a rotary pizza slicer and a salad to share.

"Can you do the honours?" Emma said. "I can't cut it without triggering the PTSD of you-know-who screaming *pizza slice* at me."

Chloe set about rolling the slicer this way and that.

"So, it didn't work out staying at Leon's," she said.

"Well, no. I should have seen that coming."

"Hmm," Chloe nodded. She scooped some salad onto her plate and dressed it with oil and balsamic vinegar. Emma did the same.

"I'm sorry you didn't have a great holiday," Chloe said.

"Well, I'm just feeling a bit lost, Chloe. I came here with Kendal, who I've been with for two years on and off."

"The Disney prince guy?" Chloe said.

"Disney villain," Emma said. "I caught him in bed with the chalet maid."

Chloe gasped.

"Literally in bed?"

"Yes. And the first thing that went through his head was to check his phone to figure out why my location was still on the slopes. Like it was a failure in technology. *Who can I sue?*"

"Wow."

Chloe ate her pizza with a knife and fork, cutting it into neat triangles accompanied by a salad leaf. Emma placed the slice in her hand back onto her plate and unwrapped her cutlery. After a week with Leon, preparing for the real world required rehabilitation.

"So, he was tracking you?" Chloe asked.

"Yes. Except I had dropped my phone, so he thought he had all the time in the world. In our bed, by the way."

"Two years. But, Emma, you don't seem so upset."

"I was at first. Horrified. I was out on the cold street with my belongings in a bin liner, and Leon took me in."

"And how was that?"

Emma paused, and absent-mindedly pinched her chin as she thought. She stared up at a green bottle that hung from the ceiling alongside dried ropes of garlic and pewter mugs. A waiter approached the table, and Chloe shook her head before he had a chance to speak.

"I don't know what to think, Chloe," Emma admitted, finally. "I suppose I feel a bit stupid about the whole thing."

She wiped her eyes with the back of her hand, and Chloe dug around in her purse for a tissue.

"What *whole thing*?"

"Leon and I got close. And I freaked out. The thing is, my career is really important to me and right now I've got an urgent case. I need to be back in London, focusing on that. I should be getting a promotion."

"How did you leave it with Leon?" Chloe asked.

Emma settled her knife and fork on her plate and wiped her lips on her napkin. In the most polite but guarded way, she said, "Chloe, if I talk about Leon, it makes me emotional. I don't know what's wrong with me."

"Oh, sorry," Chloe said, reaching across the table and clasping Emma's hand.

"There's me being incredibly nosey. Tell me about this promotion!" Chloe said.

Emma smiled, back on dry land after a floundering swim.

"So, there's this huge Swiss corporation, you might have heard of them..."

"Thank you. You won't regret it," Emma fawned, ending the call and tossing her phone onto the bed. She spun herself round on the chair in her room and gave a yelp of excitement, tapping out a message to her mum.

'AMAZING news. I've been promoted to client lead for the new Swiss firm. We got it! Was warned it will be a significant step up. Looking forward to the challenge.'

Emma said the last few words to see how they sounded out loud. The challenge. An email arrived from her boss and she scrolled through it in a blur to reread the number he had dropped on the phone. Divided into twelve, it made a sumptuous monthly salary.

She wanted to tell someone, but who? Her dad and brother didn't need her showing off, and would only worry about her stress levels. Kendal would have shrugged and asked if that number was good or bad. There was Leon, of course. She wondered what he might think, and could only picture the broken expression on his face as he washed up their coffee mugs for the last time. In anticipation of the increased stress of her new role, she ordered a book on mindfulness. A few minutes later, she cancelled that order and bought it as an audiobook instead, which she could listen to at the gym. It was all about living in the moment, apparently. Surely, she could do that and work out at the same time?

A clean start was what was needed. She would return to London with a smile on her face, fill her flat with rustic oak furniture and work as late as she pleased. She was single now, with no aspirations to see a silly ballet about a swan. Life would be simple, as it had been at university. Head down and undistracted by relationship drama.

With that in mind, she turned off her bedside light and closed her eyes. She tried to picture her new look, stepping out of a taxi in a sharp, graphite grey suit. But all she could think about were swans and their great wings, sweeping into the air and disappearing into the horizon.

Chapter Twenty-Four

♥

"So did you come for ski rental, or because this is the one spot that Leon won't step foot in," Chloe asked.

Emma sighed, and kissed Chloe on both cheeks, European style.

"I did come to pick up some skis for the morning, if that's okay?"

"Of course. Help yourself," said Chloe.

Emma found the equipment that she had borrowed earlier in the week and slid her hiking boots into a wooden cubby hole. She took out her wallet, but Chloe waved it away. She stood to wiggle her heel into the moulded plastic, then sat down to do up the countless buckles.

"I was moping around in my room, trying to read contracts on my phone screen. I thought, this is crazy. Today is my last chance to ski for who knows how long."

"Are you flying this evening?"

"Yes," Emma replied. "Not until 8pm, so I can at least ski until lunch. Has Kendal been in, by the way?"

"Ah, the Disney villain. No. Are you avoiding him too?"

Emma walked to the ski rack and picked out her skis.

"Not *avoiding* him, exactly. Yes. A little bit. I'm making a fresh start."

She opened the door to leave, triggering the ring of a little cow bell. Chloe gave a smile and a little wave.

The area at the top of the slope was less busy than it had been since she'd arrived. It was Monday, and most European kids were back in school. The queues for the lifts were non-existent, and Emma cruised confidently to the turnstile, flashed her wrist and skated through. She stood alone on the conveyor belt and looked over her shoulder in anticipation of the chairlift to scoop her up. What had been a terrifying ordeal just days ago gave her a delightful floaty feeling in her stomach. She thought of being in the back of the car and screaming in delight as her parents drove over a humpback bridge. Emma looked at the empty bench seat beside her and imagined her mum there. She closed her eyes and tried to picture her face and hear what she had to say. She smiled.

The chairlift began to steepen in its ascent, and she recognised the jagged forest beneath her feet. Emma peered down, hoping to see the hole she had dug to rescue her phone. She laughed at the thought of Leon shouting 'stop!' when he saw the flash of black being flung from the spade.

Memories of that pre-dawn hike came flooding back, and a tear formed in the corner of her eye, rolling down until it was absorbed by the spongy rim of her goggles. She ignored it, as if she might keep it a secret even from her other eye. But soon she was bawling, and had no choice but to prop her eyewear onto forehead and wipe the tears onto the back of her mittens. Her phone pinged and she reached for it, but paused when she remembered what happened last time.

The lift neared its destination, and she raised the bar, pulling her goggles back down to dismount.

At the top of the piste she was alone. The valleys were quiet except for the metallic clunk as the chairlift cable wrapped around a huge wheel and began its journey back down the mountain. From this altitude, Emma could barely make out individual buildings in the town. Just the spire of the church and the gondola station with its brutalist concrete roof. She gripped a mitten between her teeth and pulled it from her hand, hoping for a text. There were no new messages, but she saw a notification symbol on an app she didn't recognise at first.

Emma tapped the icon and remembered the wildlife camera she had bought for Leon. There were two videos; one of Leon acting like a bear, and a new one with a timestamp around 3am. Leon's hen house was a bright oblong against pitch darkness. Skulking into shot from the bottom right was an animal, bright white and ghostly. It ran up the face of the coop, like a splash of liquid. Emma immediately knew it wasn't a fox. She considered a stoat or marten, but this animal was not lithe, but solid. She took a screenshot and zoomed in, examining its massive paws and tufted ears. It was feline, but nothing like Jas. It was bigger than any domestic cat she had seen, and its tail was little more than a black stub. A lynx? Surely not. The animal got to the roof of the enclosure and paused, staring momentarily at the camera with eyes that looked like white lasers. It must have got spooked, because it leaped to the ground – a distance of over ten feet – and disappeared into the forest. The whole video lasted twenty seconds, and Emma watched it a dozen times.

Leon would have found it mesmerising, but the very thought of him dragged her back to a place she wanted to escape. With just hours to go until she left this town, it made sense to focus on the future, not what happened at Leon's cabin last night, or the night before that. She sat on the snow and stared out onto the cloudless sky. It was blissfully serene, but instead of soaking it up, her mind swirled with images of London life. The cold white glow of her screen as the office cleaner hoovered around her feet. No more moping, she thought. You've made your bed, and now you have to lie in it.

She opened up the long thread of messages to her mum, scrolling back through countless updates and photos. It had to stop, she thought, and her future had to start now. That's what her mum believed in. Checklists and action. She was an emotional wreck, and it was time to get a hold of herself.

'*Mum, this is the last message I'm going to send you. You know how I tell you everything is great? It isn't. Switzerland is awful. Kendal ditched me for the chalet host. Leon turned out to be a rebound fling. But I don't want to go home, either. My career is like a spin class that never ends. London has like, one tree, and drunk men wee on it. And I'm mad. I've texted you every day for ten years. It needs to stop. Now. I love you. But this isn't good for me. I know you would understand. Over and out.*'

By the time she hit send, she was crying her eyes out and her bum was numb from the cold snow. She swiped left on the whole thread of messages and the red button marked Delete popped up. She used one thumb to push the other to tap it, consigning thousands of messages and photos to the virtual dustbin. Her A-level certificates atop a freshly torn envelope. First boyfriends. Grainy photos of university days, London life. All of it, gone.

She skied as best she could but struggled to commit to her turns. She could almost hear Leon tapping his poles together, chasing her down the slope and screaming psychopathic threats that he would enact when he caught her. She looked back for him and hated herself for doing so. He was like the lynx, bursting into frame with a flash of masculine beauty before disappearing into the shadows.

Cruising down a gentle blue run that weaved through pretty woods, she heard her name being shouted from the lift. Leon! She pulled over to the edge of the run, remembering his advice to find a flat area where she would remain visible to incoming skiers. She skidded to a stop at the side of the slope, where the manicured ribbons of snow gave way to the dark woods beyond. Staring back at the lift, all she could make out was the distant silhouettes of skiers against the bright white sky. At the foot of the run was a restaurant, which she made her way down to. She ordered a hot chocolate and suppressed her gathering excitement.

"Hello stranger," came a familiar voice.

With a sinking feeling in her stomach, she looked up.

"Hello Kendal."

Chapter Twenty-Five

"May I?" he asked.

Kendal looked around for a server and raised a hand. "Vin chaud," he mouthed. "Two."

"I'm good," Emma said.

"I know."

He looked at Emma, studying the contours of her face as if he hadn't seen her for months. His self-satisfied grin held no hint of remorse, only the predatory look of a wolf.

"You look beautiful," he said. "With your panda eyes."

"What do you want, Kendal?" Emma said. She toyed with her empty mug and regretted not having ordered something stronger. Like an axe, or a gun.

A waitress dropped off two glasses of warm red wine, which Kendal slid to his side of the table.

"I want for nothing," he said. "But I am glad we got this chance to catch up. Clear the air."

She breathed in through her nose and out through her lips. It didn't help the gathering pace of her heartbeat.

"I'm sorry, okay?" he said. "I just, was on holiday. And we hadn't been getting on. You know that? It wasn't working."

Emma moved her chair back a little but realised she was cornered against a wooden balustrade.

"What you did was awful, Kendal. Inexcusable."

"I didn't say it wasn't," he said, raising both his hands in the air.

"Mea culpa," he said. "I got swept away in the moment and I shouldn't have. It wasn't fair on you, and I'm sorry."

"And you and Alice? What happened with her?" Emma asked.

He laughed.

"Nothing *happened* with her. We didn't say another word about it. I was deeply embarrassed, of course, and so was she."

"I just don't believe anything that comes out of your mouth anymore, Kendal."

"What would I get from lying to you, Em? We're not together anymore."

"So did you sleep with Alice again? Be honest."

"No," he said, with a shocked look on his face. Emma waited, and Kendal moved onto his second glass. "I mean, we *might* have, last night. Yes. But you had made it very clear we were over."

"Two years, we were together. To suggest that I should have seen it coming because the magic was gone. I was trying to fix it. You could have at least talked to me about how you were feeling."

"I'm sorry, Emma. You're right. I'm not cut out for relationships."

"Why are you drinking at noon?" she asked. "We've got to catch a flight tonight."

"Well *mother*, I'm celebrating," he said, leaning on the table and fixing her with his gaze. "Remember I told you about the building investment?"

"You mentioned you were looking at a chalet or something," Emma said.

"It's a whole building. Six apartments, parking, boot room. And your new boyfriend has finally signed on the dotted line.

So, I'm celebrating. Preemptively, I should say. I'm due down there after this drink."

"Leon?"

"Yes, old Muller. He has sold his plot, at bloody last. Been negotiating with that fool for months, and he waited until the very last day."

Emma narrowed her eyes, and Kendal continued.

"He has a deadline, so we knew he had to get the deal done this week unless he found another buyer. Which I'm kind of amazed he didn't."

"So that's why you had to be here this week?" Emma said. "To sign a contract."

"No, no. Not at all. I came here for your birthday. But it's a happy coincidence. Two birds, and all that."

Emma raised her eyebrows.

"Poor choice of words," he said.

"So, Leon sold his cabin?" Emma asked.

"Yes. You stayed in it, I hear? Ramshackle pile of sticks, isn't it? A bloody wolf could blow it down. Beautiful plot though. Will be worth a fortune when we're done with it."

Emma said. "Where's he going to live?"

"Who cares. You know about his debt, right?"

"Not really. He's quite a private person," Emma said.

"Well, I got the full scoop this morning. He sank a lot of money into medical care for his sister. He's in a lot of debt, hence the literal yard sale."

"Whatever it takes," Emma muttered.

"Huh?"

"He did whatever it took. Would you do that, for someone you love?" she asked pointedly.

Kendal screwed up his face.

"Sure. I'd write the cheque. What's your point?"

"He didn't just write a cheque. He sacrificed everything he had. And you'll end up even richer, and he'll end up losing everything. Because his sister got sick."

"Well, whatever," Kendal said. He pushed the dregs of his second vin chaud away and poked his tongue in and out like a snake. "Shouldn't have had the second one. Bit much."

Emma couldn't hear him. Her head was in her hands, fingers squeezing at her temples as she thought.

"Anyway, what I wanted to say was; no hard feelings," Kendal said, reaching across the table and touching her hair. She ignored him, and he continued.

"I got fifty miles an hour, today." He shoved his screen into her field of view.

"I'm happy for you," she said, slinging it back like a hockey puck.

"It's so much better now the kids have gone back to school. Slopes are empty. Charlie and I were flying. You know that feeling when...well, you probably don't. But when you're going faster and faster, and there's the point where you couldn't turn even if you wanted to. That's a rush, Em. It really is."

She looked up toward Kendal, but stared right through him.

"That's...my life," she said.

He looked behind himself to see what she was fixated on, but saw only a wall. Emma's mouth drifted open as she sunk deeper into thought.

"I *do* know that feeling," she continued, eyes widening.. "Of hurtling faster and faster until I feel sick. Until every muscle in my body is tense and burning, and I'm trying to hold on. Trying to grin and bear it. That's me and you, Kendal."

He sat back on his chair, his eyebrows furrowed.

"Bit harsh," he said.

"It's what I do," she said, wide-eyed, and palms flat against her cheeks. "I just...hurtle into the abyss. I convince myself it's because I've chosen that path, but I haven't. I've built up momentum and I'm too scared to slam on the brakes, or even change course. And the world rushes by in such a blur that I forget that it's even there. I don't see the other paths. Other jobs. Other partners. Instead I keep staring forward and hanging on for dear life. It's you and me. It's corporate law. I can't do that anymore."

Emma's hands were on her forehead, her chestnut hair spilling through the gaps between her fingers.

Kendal looked at her as if she had gone mad. He pocketed his phone, somewhat regretful of mentioning his speed record.

"Well, when we get back, you are always welcome to come over. My friends are your friends," he said.

She looked him in the eye, and shook her head slowly.

"I'm not going back."

"Well, you are. Our flight leaves in eight hours."

"I can't have my London life *and* Leon. I can only have one or the other. And I've chosen the wrong one."

Emma jumped to her feet and became tangled between the table and her chair, which she eventually shoved onto its side in frustration. She stumbled as hastily as she could in her cumbersome boots, out of the door and across the snowy deck. Kendal chased after her.

"What are you doing?" he asked.

"Whatever it takes," she said, wrestling her skis from the rack.

"Why?" Kendal called out.

Emma slapped them onto the snow and kicked her boots into the bindings.

"He shouldn't have to sell his family's land for a damn medical bill," she said. "There must be another way."

"What's it to you?" Kendal asked. "He's just a bloody ski instructor."

He seemed agitated, blocking her way.

"He's not just a ski instructor, Kendal. He's a wonderful guy with a heart of gold. That place has his childhood in it. His chickens. His whole life. Has he signed already?"

She threaded her mittens through the loops on her poles, then pushed away toward a blue run that led down to town. Kendal chased for a moment and attempted to grab at Emma's jacket, but she slipped beyond his reach. He ran back, grabbed his skis and skated after her.

Neither of them heard the waitress, who waved their bill from the deck.

Kendal caught up with Emma quickly and skied alongside. She tucked her poles along the bone of her hips and sank down into a more aerodynamic pose. He shouted across at her.

"Emma, don't be ridiculous. You hardly know this guy. It's none of your business."

"Kendal, just piss off!" she screamed through gritted teeth.

Emma's skis shook as she hurtled down the slope. They dipped into the tracks left by other skiers, finding a life of their own, parting and regrouping, the plastic of her boots cracking together.

"This is not your deal to ruin, Emma!" he shouted, skiing so close that they nearly collided.

They approached a fork in the piste, where a sign pointed right for a mellow green route to town, or straight for a blue run. Emma held her nerve and blasted over the brow into the steeper, faster option. Her stomach leapt as she descended into the slope, feeling like a bar of soap plunging into a sink. Her skis chattered now, blasting through slashes of snow left by more advanced skiers capable of proper turns. Emma was now way beyond her record speed and terrified out of her mind. A couple of gentile skiers ahead of her snaked down the slope, gliding from one tree-lined side to the other. Emma hollered at them to get out of the way. "SORRRRYY!" she shouted as she clung on for dear life. Her skis, parallel and shoulder width apart, skipped over bumps and moguls. In the distance, she saw the slope mellow out, and all she could do was remain crouched and pray she made it to safety. For once, she knew where she was going.

Emma shot past a group of skiers waiting at a lift. Kendal came careering into her path and skidded to a stop, spraying snow downslope. Emma attempted to make an emergency turn, cranking the edges of her skis into the icy snow to change her trajectory. *Look at where you want to go*, she told herself. But it was impossible not to look at the smug prince in her path with his plastic hair, and she barrelled into him like a bowling ball.

Kendal was pummelled to the floor and Emma catapulted over him, landing in a tangled forward roll. In the ensuing tumble, her right ski jammed tip first into the ground. It bent like a pole vault and then sprang from her boot. It shot past Kendal, who was himself dazed and barely able to sit up. He looked downslope at Emma, already dusting herself off and attempting to clamber to her feet.

"Emma, there's nothing you can do," Kendal said.

He crawled upslope to reach for her ski. Emma, meanwhile, staggered awkwardly uphill, moving her remaining ski a few inches at a time. Step by step she approached Kendal, who remained an obstacle as he lay on the snow.

"Pass me my ski!" she said.

He looked at her, then at the blue and white ski in his hand.

"Now, Kendal!"

He stood up, with both of his poles in his left hand and her ski in his right.

"Emma, the deal is done. Just go back to London. Go home."

She reached for her ski but Kendal yanked it out of reach.

"London's not my home, Kendal. I need to see Leon."

He laughed.

"Well, this place certainly isn't your home. You wouldn't even know about it if I hadn't brought you here. This is the thanks I get."

She swiped at her ski, but Kendal launched it into the woods like a javelin. It sailed between trees and landed deep in the frozen undergrowth.

"What the fuck? Kendal!"

Emma looked into the trees, unable to even see it. She looked down the slope at the town, which was perhaps a mile or two down a blue run. She pointed her single ski downhill and pushed with her right boot, as if she were skateboarding. Her momentum built until the ground rushed beneath her too quickly to risk putting her foot down. With a bent knee, her boot hovered above the snow. She jabbed her poles in to keep balance as she picked up speed.

"Emma, that's lethal. Stop!" Kendal cried.

She focused on the trees to the right of the slope and carved a great arc toward it, before twisting her shoulders and focusing on the left. Don't look down, she told herself. Her left calf burned from controlling that single ski, fighting to keep it straight. Her right thigh became an agonising cramp as she held her heavy boot off the ground.

After a few fraught minutes, she crested a piste and looked down to see the base of the gondola. Unable to make a controlled stop, she aimed for a quiet patch of snow and hoped for the best, flying downslope on one leg. She shot past the coffee kiosk and queues of impressed beginners waiting for the uplift. As she approached the part where the snow thinned out to meet the road, she swung her ski to the side and made an emergency stop. In front of a bewildered group of kids awaiting their instructor, Emma crashed to the floor and slid on her side to a stop.

She kicked off her remaining ski and stabbed her poles into the snow. She abandoned them all and ran toward the town square.

Chapter Twenty-Six

E mma burst through the door of the estate agent.

"Where is Leon?" she asked.

"He is celebrating, I expect," the realtor said. He lifted up a couple of sheets of paper with dense text.

Emma's heart sank. She knew, at least, where to find him.

"Table for one?" asked the server at Caspers, menu in hand.

Emma looked over his shoulder toward the bar area and spotted Leon, perched on a stool and hunched over an empty glass. She rushed over.

"Leon, I'm sorry," she said, putting her arm on his shoulder.

He shrugged it off. Emma pulled up a stool alongside him.

"I said some awful things," she said, softly.

"I really don't need this today," Leon said.

"I know about your cabin. About the bills you have to clear. I'm so sorry, about all of it. And the way I walked out, after all you did for me."

Leon stared down at an empty glass. His hat was on the bar and his hair hung down, hiding his eyes.

"It's okay," he said. "Did you manage to fix your job, at least?"

"Leon, I like things to be orderly, and planned. At least, I thought I did. You came into my life like a meteor and turned it upside down, and I freaked out," Emma said, pulling his chin so he would face her. Her fingers touching his face electrified them both. Memories of their time together in the cabin came flooding back.

"You are nothing like Kendal. Not one bit," she said.

He looked away, fiddling with a beer mat.

"Talk to me!" Emma begged.

"I don't know what to say," he replied. "You fly home tonight. I spent the last 24 hours trying to deal with that, and thinking about what I'm going to do now that I don't have a home."

"Am I crazy for feeling the way I do about you?" she said.

"And how is that?"

"I'm falling in love with you, Leon. I feel sick with dread at the thought of my life in London. And it's not the city, it's you. I can't face never seeing you again. I couldn't help wanting my phone to ring. And now I know I don't want to walk away from you."

He looked at her with his doleful blue eyes.

"Please, talk to me," she said.

Leon sighed.

"Emma, you know my sister died last year. And since then, things have been difficult. I've been...depressed," he said, as though the word fell short of everything he had experienced. "It's like being underwater. People talk and I can only hear muffled sounds. Friends want me to see them but all I want is to be in the dark. On the mountain, I manage to forget. No, not forget, but it's not in the front of my mind. I ski, come here and talk to friends. Music, dancing, and I feel good. But eventually I have to walk back to my cabin and I think of Sophie and the loneliness. And I do it all over again the next day. I can't even face going inside that shop. That was her thing."

"I'm so sorry, Leon. That must be awful."

"But this week, I felt like I burst out of the water. I was free. I woke up happy every day. Hiking, tobogganing, skating. You made me feel alive. That morning I was in the chicken house, I was actually thinking that I would clear out Sophie's room, finally. I wanted to make it so you could come back for weekends and holidays. I wanted to show you how beautiful this place is in summer, when the cows are grazing on the slopes, and we could hike and bike. Swim in crystal clear lakes."

"Then I left," she said.

He nodded, reliving the despair of abandonment.

"It's too late now," he said. "Your flight leaves tonight, and it's taking every last bit of strength to get through today. Sophie is gone. You'll go, and my cabin goes. I can't even keep my chickens. Everything I love is going away."

"Leon, would you try to make it work, with me?"

He lifted his head up.

"Long distance relationships are hard, Emma. Harder than close distance relationships, and even those ones are quite hard."

"I don't mean long distance. What if I don't go home?" she said. "What if I stay here. You, me, Jas the cat and your chickens."

He raised an eyebrow.

"Seriously?" he said. "What about your job?"

"I hate my job, Leon. I could find work here in town or doing consulting online."

"What's consulting?"

"Doesn't matter," she said. "What do you think?"

He put his hands on her shoulders.

"Emma, don't talk about this stuff if you don't mean it. I cried the other day for the first time since I lost Sophie. Are you actually serious about moving to Switzerland?"

She reached into her jacket and unzipped the inside pocket. Her hand emerged with a slip of white card, with the airport codes for Zurich and London. Emma pinched it and tore it into two neat strips. Leon smiled so hard he lit up the room.

He gripped her cheeks with his strong hands and pulled her face toward his. They stared into each other's eyes.

"I really do love you, Emma. You're the most interesting and beautiful person I have ever met. I know it's crazy to say it this early."

Emma yelped with excitement and kissed him.

"Right. What's the deal with your cabin?" she asked.

Leon reached into his jacket and pulled out a few sheets of paper, triple folded and stapled in the corner. Emma smoothed them out on the bar with her forearm and scanned through it.

"I sold it," Leon said. "To your ex. Crazy huh? I had no choice. I have a few months to pack up and find something new."

"This deal is between you and Kendal," she said.

"I know. And I've signed it already. It's gone, Emma."

Emma pulled out her phone and tapped on the ill-fated 'Find my Friends' app.

"What are you looking for?" Leon asked, peering at the screen.

"Kendal," she said.

"Already?"

"You've signed it, Leon. *He* hasn't. Not yet."

"There he is!" Emma said, spotting Kendal coasting over the brow of the hill.

"How can you tell that's him?" Leon asked.

"He's got three skis. Don't ask. Look, wait at Caspers. If it's you and me versus Kendal, it'll become a big cock-waving battle. I know how to deal with him."

"Deal with him how?" said Leon. "What are you trying to achieve?"

"Do you trust me?" she said.

"Of course. Good luck."

Leon stepped out of sight and Emma jogged over to where Kendal stopped. He passed her missing ski.

"Took bloody ages to find this. I've got quite the throw," he said, proudly.

"Thanks," she said, with a mock smile. "That's so kind of you to retrieve the ski you launched into a forest."

Kendal stamped down on the backs of his bindings and slotted his together base to base. He swung them across his shoulder, poles hanging from the tips. He looked at Emma, still holding her lone ski.

"Is there something else?" he asked.

"Yes. There is," she began, walking alongside him. "I don't think you should fund this development."

He sucked through his teeth.

"Why, because of lover boy? Emma, I can't back out now, even if I wanted to. Anyway, he needs the money."

Kendal walked toward town with Emma hurrying alongside.

"Well, you haven't signed it, so you absolutely could back out if you wanted to," she said.

"And why would I?" he said. "It's a rock solid opportunity. I write a cheque, someone does some work. Tap tap. Bang bang. We sell five of the apartments and I keep the sixth for myself."

"The deal is great on paper," she said. "It's just that you're being ripped off."

He raised his eyebrows. They turned the corner to the town square.

"I'm not Leon," he said. "I am more than capable of assessing a business deal."

"I want to show you something," she said, holding out her phone.

He waved it away.

"Emma, to be honest I've had enough fun and games this morning. Traipsing around a damn wood looking for your ski was a project I didn't need. And that wine is giving me a headache."

He leaned his skis against the glass window of the estate agent. They clattered to the floor, and he left them in a heap as he greeted the realtor.

"Goodbye, Emma," Kendal said. "I'll see you on the plane. I've got some business to attend to."

Kendal clunked into the shop in his heavy ski boots, and Emma followed him in. Desks were shaped like aeroplane wings, and on one was a model of Leon's plot of land. Emma recognised the steep slope which she had sledged down, and the pond out front. Between them was no trace of a log cabin, just a car park with little people carrying skis. A three-storey building loomed over the area where the chicken coop once stood, all glass balconies and sharp angles. Kendal reached in, God-like, and plucked a tiny model of a man holding skis.

"That's me," he said.

Emma thrust her screen in front of him.

"Do you know what that is?" she asked.

"An iPhone ten," he said, grimacing. "No wonder you stole mine."

"Not the phone, what's on it!" Emma said.

Kendal took it from her and peered at the image.

"Ok, it's a cat video. I don't have time for memes. Forward it to me, though. Let the adults take care of business now, please."

The property developer reopened the door. He pursed his lips and upturned the palm of his hand, as if to waft her out. Emma ignored him.

"Kendal, that's a lynx. There are only 150 in the whole of Europe. Fiercely protected," she said.

He shrugged.

"It's on Leon's land. The land you're about to buy."

"Great. I'll start a zoo," he joked.

The realtor peered over Kendal's shoulder, watching the video loop over and over.

"You'll start nothing because they'll never let you build so much as a sold sign," Emma said. "You'll be bogged down by environmental surveys and red tape for years. It's going to be an exact repeat of that manor house you bought with the bats. Which as I recall, is still an empty shell, four years later."

"Please, madam," the realtor said. "With due respect, this is a deal we have been working on for some time. If we need to do additional surveys and assessments, that is in the course of business. Now if I could ask you to leave."

Kendal crouched beside the model and brushed a hand over the white sloping roof. He looked at Emma, who was holding her phone, its screen flashing against her salopettes.

"I don't like this," Kendal said.

The property developer gripped the pen so hard that the top popped off. He flapped the papers in Kendal's face.

"For six months we've been negotiating this deal," he said. "This man, Muller, doesn't have legal representation. He has a woman with a photo of a cat. That is not a reason to back out of the deal of a lifetime."

"He *does* have legal representation," Emma said calmly. "He has me. Yes, I am a woman. Yes, I have a photo of a cat. Here's the thing. It's not just a cat, and I'm not just a woman. It's a critically endangered species with special legal protection. And I'm his lawyer, and I will fight you tooth and nail to stop your spade going into that earth."

Kendal whistled. The exasperated realtor thrust the papers toward him with an outstretched arm. Kendal snatched them and tossed them to the floor like a dead pigeon.

"Stop flapping those bloody papers at me!" he said. "It's over. Can't you see that?"

The developer's mouth fell open. "Over? It hasn't started. You can't back out now! I've spent months putting this deal together."

"There will be other deals, I'm sure. I'm not going to spend the next two years fighting the woman with the picture of a cat."

"Why not?" he said.

"Because she won't lose. We will."

Kendal walked to the door and shouldered it open, holding it for Emma. She passed through, barely able to contain her grin. The developer was left standing by the model, the veins pulsing on his temples.

Chapter Twenty-Seven

♥

Leon was perusing flats to rent in the window of a rival estate agent when he spotted Emma across the town square. He jogged over, putting his hands on her cheeks and delicately kissing the bridge of her nose.

"How did it go?" he asked.

" I've got good news."

Emma sat on the bench and patted. Leon took his cue, nestling in beside.

"I convinced Kendal to not sign the deal. So you still have your cabin," she said.

Leon's eyes narrowed.

"Wait. You went in there and torpedoed my deal?"

She bared her teeth.

"Yes. That's good, isn't it? We love that cabin. And the chickens. Swan lake."

Leon leaned forward with his elbows on his knees and his head hung low.

"That place is my life. But Emma, I have this crazy bill. I have to pay it. You know that."

"Don't worry, I've got an idea," she said. "I'll give up my flat in London and pay rent to you, which you can use to pay off your bill. In time, we'll consider co-owning or whatever. But for now, we can live together in the cabin and get back on our feet."

"So, I get to keep you. And we're going to live together at *our* house?" he said.

"Yes. With Jas and the chickens and a lynx. Are you crying?" she laughed.

"I may have something in my eye," he said.

"Nigel, I've been thinking about the job offer," Emma said. "I'm going to politely decline."

"What did you say? I think I misheard."

"Decline," she repeated.

"You can't. Is it the money?"

Emma looked out of the window of Leon's ski shop. She was dreading this call, but she always attacked a to-do list in order of dread. Her mum had taught her that.

"No. I'm taking a break. I am actually handing in my notice," she said.

The line was quiet. Outside, Leon crouched to adjust a kid's ski boot.

"No, Emma," Nigel said, in a voice that appeared calm and patient – patronising, even – but simmered with rage. "This client just signed with us because they liked the work you did. I've told them you're their contact at our firm. You can't do this to me."

"I'll work out my notice remotely so you can find another client lead," she said.

"Remotely?" he spat.

Such was Nigel's aversion to remote working, that during the pandemic he had sent an email stating that he'd rather people came to work dead than work from home.

"The work I did so far for that client, I did remotely," Emma said. "And they liked it."

"I need you back in the office," he said. "ASAP."

"Nigel, this isn't negotiable."

"Everything's negotiable," he said.

"Not me. I'm living in Switzerland. I can even go to visit the client, if you like. But I'm not coming back to London."

"Why did you wait until today to spring this on me?" he said.

"I didn't know."

"Oh really, you just decided on a whim to move to Switzerland? Have you lost your mind?"

She watched Leon patiently waiting on the pavement outside, shopping bags swinging from his hands. He caught her eye through the window and attempted a pirouette, but a paper bag split and apples spilled onto the snow. Emma suppressed a laugh and turned away from him.

"I haven't lost my mind. I want to try something different. This is me, giving you my notice, Nigel."

"My flight takes off in two minutes," Emma said.

"You won't make it," Leon replied, tossing some shallots in a pan.

"I knew you'd say that," she replied.

"So, what do we do about the lynx?" he said. "I don't like my chickens being out there with this cat."

He watched the video on Emma's phone for the hundredth time.

"I'll set the alerts so we get a notification when the camera is triggered. Then you can run out and chase it off."

"You can," he countered. "I'm not going out to fight that thing in my boxer shorts. Its paws are like tennis rackets!"

"You're a great big chicken," she teased. "I'm surprised it hasn't come inside for you."

Leon put his hands on Emma's shoulders and kissed her neck.

"You're funny, Emma. Tomorrow I'm going to have a clear out," he said. "It's time. I feel ready. Will you help me?"

She placed a loving hand on his.

"Of course I'll help. And then we're going to get Wifi at the house." "What's Wifi?" he asked.

Emma slung a bin liner into the back of Leon's pickup truck, but it tumbled back down, tripped over the tailgate and bowled into her chest. Leon smiled but his mind was elsewhere. He passed her the hook of a long orange strap, and together they hauled it over the top of the load. Emma ratcheted it down until the bags of clothes looked set to be cleaved in two. She turned her attention to shovelling snow from around the tyres while Leon disconnected the battery charger that snaked from the bonnet to the kitchen window.

"Moment of truth," he said, fingers crossed.

The starter motor whined, pleading with the heavy cylinders to roll into life. After a few nerve-wracking seconds, the engine fired up for the first time all winter. The chickens watched the commotion from the outdoor part of their enclosure.

Emma returned to Sophie's old room to find Leon placing a photograph on the windowsill. Jasmine sniffed around the empty built-in wardrobes, and Emma scooped her up and kissed her soft grey fur. All that remained in the room was the bed, mattress and some ski equipment leaning against the wall. Leon had even removed the curtains and rug.

"Are you sure you want me to keep the ice skates and skis?" Emma said.

"I'm sure," he replied, reaching an arm around her shoulder. "Sophie was big on recycling things. And it's kind of cool that her skates will skate on, and her skis will make fresh tracks in the snow. She would have loved that. She would have wanted you to have them, for sure."

Emma put her boot onto the metal step and hauled herself into the cabin of the truck, its bench seat so cold she wished she'd brought a cushion. Leon solemnly clunked it into gear and the pickup crawled across the front yard, its rock-solid suspension sharing every rut and bump. The smell of diesel and agricultural rumble of the engine took Emma back to being out on the tractor with her dad, long after her friends would have been tucked up in bed.

"Are you okay?" he asked.

"I'm good," she said.

The truck bounced down a dirt track, branches whipping at its mirrors, until they joined a two-lane road which would take them to the valley floor. The views were breathtaking, and eventually Emma stopped panicking as Leon threaded the truck around hairpin bends. It was a serene, still day, with a slight sparkle to the air as the sun lit snow dusting from the trees.

"How are you feeling?" she asked.

He shrugged.

"I'm okay. I'm actually doing much better than I thought I would. I've been putting this off for a year, and part of me is thinking 'What took you so long?' But I didn't have you. That's what took so long. I literally couldn't have done this without you. You saved me. You really did."

He looked lovingly at Emma and reached over to move some hair away from her face. She took his wrist and gently, but urgently, placed it back on the steering wheel.

"She got sick so fast," he said.

Emma nodded.

"My sister," he added, unnecessarily.

"I know," she said. "I saw some photos when we were clearing up. I'm so sorry."

He sighed and toyed with his lower lip as he thought.

"It's okay. We have to move forward, because that's what they would have wanted. My sister didn't want me moping around, hiding in bars, keeping her bedroom door shut. She would have thought that was dumb. I did this drive every day when she was in hospital in Zurich. One time, toward the end, she looked horrendous. Skin like porcelain. Wires. Tubes. Machines beeping. She saw the way I looked at her, and she just shrugged and said 'shit happens'." Leon smiled at the memory and shook his head. "Can you believe that? She was a badass."

As Leon spoke about Sophie, life, and even death, Emma felt his energy return. As they worked their way through switchbacks and tunnels, the road that connected his village to the rest of the world became more than just the route to a hospital in Zurich.

"Look up there!" he said, leaning across Emma to point to a steep slope beside the road.

"Leon, please look at the road," she said, stabbing at an invisible brake in her footwell.

"Me and my friends built a kicker there and jumped this road," he said proudly.

"Kicker?"

"Like a giant cheese wedge of snow. Then we waited for our other buddy to drive the morning bakery delivery up. He was all tired and groggy, and suddenly two skiers jumped the road in front of him. It was awesome."

He looked wild and manic, glancing over to Emma to taste her reaction. She couldn't care less about his stunts but watching the colour return to his cheeks was like seeing her phone come back to life after two nights of being buried in the snow. She tapped his thigh.

"I'm very impressed. You got the girl. No need to *ever* do that again."

"Next time, we'll do it together," he grinned.

At the foot of the hill, they joined a highway that took them to the store where they would donate Sophie's clothing and belongings. Furniture shops and drive through restaurants were dotted along the road, and it reminded Emma of a world she had forgotten existed. Even seeing cars felt strange, after so many weeks in the village.

"What do you want to do with the second bedroom?" Leon asked.

"I'm not sure," she said. "It would be useful to have a place to work, I suppose. Keep the bed for when people stay over?"

"You could have Kendal to stay," he said. "You know that, right?"

Emma shuffled in her seat.

"You what?" she said. "Kendal...my ex?"

Leon looked at her with soft, loving eyes.

"Yes. He liked skiing, and I feel a bit bad that I backed out of that deal. He could come and stay. No hard feelings, right?"

"Have you lost your mind? Do you think I want Kendal round for a sleepover? He shagged the chalet host on our second day of holiday."

"Well, boys will be boys," Leon muttered.

He flicked on his indicator to pull into the Salvation Army store. Emma's face screwed up as she processed the idea of Kendal invading her lovely home. Leon backed the truck into a parking space and shut off the engine.

"I mean, Alice could stay too," he said, with a neutral shrug.

She gasped and they locked eyes. Leon couldn't keep a straight face and burst into laughter. He jumped down from the cabin, by which point Emma had already raced around to his side. He backed away with his hands up.

"Okay, okay. Then how about a cat flap for the lynx?" he said.

"Another great idea, Leon. Except I already invited Chloe to move in," she said, hands on hips.

"No," he said, throwing his head back. "Not Chloe!"

"Yep, Chloe is moving in. And the weaselly estate agent with his little white model."

"Truce," he said, flopping down the tailgate to begin unloading.

Epilogue

♥

"That's it!" Emma shouted, clapping her mittens together with a thwump.

He skidded to a stop in front of her.

"This is brilliant," he beamed. "I'm getting the hang of it."

"I never thought I'd teach my dad to ski," Emma said.

"I have to say, I never thought you'd be living in Switzerland. But I can see why you swapped lawyering for this. No contest, your honour," Michael said.

Her dad motioned out to the groomed piste, cold blue in the shadows and slashed with spears of yellow where the sun broke through the trees.

"It's so beautiful here," he said.

They watched Leon chase Emma's niece down the beginner slope. Cassie screamed with joy as she zigzagged through the soft snow, out of reach of the T-rex.

"I'm not joking, dad; that's how he taught me, too."

"I like Leon," Michael said. "He's a good one."

Emma leaned her head into her father's shoulder.

"Thanks for coming out," she said. "I knew you'd love it here."

"I don't know how you get anything done," he said.

"Well, I haven't, yet. I work a few shifts in the rental shop. Mostly I've been sorting out the flat and putting it on the market."

"And skiing, obviously. How often do you go skiing?" he asked.

"Every day. Skiing, skating, hiking. It's like being a kid again."

"I'm so happy for you, Emma. Because when you were a kid, you grew up a bit too fast. So now you're a grown up, it's good that you're being a kid again."

She smiled and watched Leon chasing Cassie. He caught up with her and lifted her up, causing her to squeal with laughter.

"What about him? Is he ever going to grow up?" she said.

Michael laughed.

"Let's hope not."

Acknowledgements

I hope you enjoyed reading Ski Lovers. I had a blast writing it. As you can probably guess, I am passionate about the mountains and have been skiing and snowboarding all my life. Never jumped a road, though.

This is the first romcom I've written, although there's a romantic undercurrent to my previous book, Hotel Taurus. That's a poolside mystery set in Crete, and although it is much darker and completely bonkers, it has some of the character of Ski Lovers. Check it out on Amazon.

It would mean the world to me if you would give Ski Lovers a review or rating on Amazon. Finally, feel free to email me directly at james@poptacular.com. Maybe you need to know if Kendal is still sleeping with Alice? (*Of course not! I mean, maybe. Okay.. .yes.*)

Lots of love to my family for all their support, to Kateryna Kirdoglo for the cover and Madeleine Rafell for editing.

James.

Printed in Great Britain
by Amazon

52237723R00133